"I never thought we'd have so much in common."

"The truth? Initially neither did I. But we do," Jack said slowly, his eyes roving over her face once again, this time with mesmerizing intensity. "Glad you came out here today?"

Lynn nodded, so aware of him she could barely breathe.

"So am I."

And then she knew. Something was happening here.

Jack knew it, too. Wordlessly he closed the distance between them, taking her by the shoulders. His head was lowering, his lips slanting over hers. She breathed in the crisp, woodsy scent of his cologne, and her palms flattened over the muscled contours of his chest, unsure of whether she was resisting or urging him on. She only knew she wanted to touch him, and that he made her feel more like a woman than she had in months.

"I told myself when I asked you out here today I wouldn't do this. I lied," he said simply. "I'm going to kiss you."

ABOUT THE AUTHOR

Cathy Gillen Thacker is a native of Ohio who now makes her home in Texas along with her three children and husband—her childhood sweetheart. A former music teacher, Cathy enjoys gardening, reading, cooking and watching movies—when she's not writing.

Books by Cathy Gillen Thacker

Perfect Match
Cathy Gillen Thacker

Harlequin Books

TORONTO • NEW YORK • LONDON
AMSTERDAM • PARIS • SYDNEY • HAMBURG
STOCKHOLM • ATHENS • TOKYO • MILAN

Published January 1989

First printing November 1988

ISBN 0-373-16277-4

Chapter One

"You want me to do *what*?" Lynn O'Brien asked incredulously. Shocked by what she'd heard, she combed her fingers restlessly through her wavy honey-blond hair and faced her old friend expectantly, waiting for her to reply.

Theresa Richards turned a dull shade of red as she met Lynn's glance. For long moments she took in Lynn's fair, freckled skin and assessing golden-brown eyes. They'd been very close once, in high school practically inseparable. Years, and careers in different professions, had made them less close, but Theresa still turned to Lynn when she was in trouble and needed a friend, someone who would try her hardest to understand.

When at last she spoke, her low voice was a barely audible murmur. "I want you to find Carter's father."

Lynn stared at her friend in consternation. In her years on the police force she'd thought she'd heard it all. Now, in her first six weeks as private investigator, she knew she hadn't even begun. "Theresa, you know there's no way the hospital would give out that kind of information voluntarily.''

"I know." Theresa stared at her friend levelly, her course of action already decided.

Lynn tried another method of reasoning with the thirty-six-year-old lab technician and mother of one four-year-old child. Theresa was small and delicate looking, but she was as strong as they came. "You agreed when you underwent the artificial insemination the donor's identity was to be kept confidential."

"And I meant it—at the time."

Lynn folded her tall frame into a chair and crossed her legs at the knees. "What's changed now?"

Theresa sighed. Without warning, tears welled up in her eyes and her voice became shaky, uneven. "Carter's been asking me about his natural father."

"You knew that would happen," she pointed out gently but firmly.

"Yes. And I'd prepared all sorts of speeches about how it didn't matter he didn't know his father, that he had a mother who loved him very much and that was enough. I believed that then, but now I'm not so sure."

Lynn could see Theresa was very troubled. "What do you mean?" she asked gently.

"Carter told me the other day that he felt like only half a person. Everyone else at his day-care center has a mother and a father. He only has a mother. He wanted to know what his daddy looked like, what he did. Lynn, I've never felt so helpless in my life. Worse,

I know how he feels. Sometimes it drives me crazy, too, not knowing anything about the person who gave him life." Theresa stopped pacing and sat down in a chair opposite Lynn.

She looked so upset, so depressed, Lynn's heart went out to her. "I'm sorry you're having a hard time," Lynn said softly. Theresa had dated a lot of men after college. Unhappily, none of these relationships had worked out and, impatient to have a family of her own, Theresa had been artificially inseminated. "Theresa," Lynn said slowly, "you aren't thinking of, well, trying to manage some sort of romance with your son's father, are you? Providing you could find him, of course."

"No." Theresa was definite about that much. "I'm not that naive. I know that his father was just a donor."

Lynn gave a silent sigh of relief. "Then why do you want me to find Carter's father?" she asked curiously, anxious to understand her friend's line of reasoning.

"I'm concerned about potential health problems."

"Wait a minute." Lynn raised a silencing palm. "I thought you *knew* the donor had no health problems—"

"He didn't at the time he donated sperm. That's not to say something hasn't developed in the past five years. For all I know, his family could now have quite a history of cancer or high blood pressure or even heart disease."

"Wouldn't the hospital tell you if this were the case?"

"If they knew about it, yes. How do I know this man is conscientious enough to have reported any new health developments in his family?"

Lynn was silent. "Okay, I understand why you're asking me to do this. And it makes sense, but I still don't think you're thinking clearly. Even if I could find the man, and I'm not at all sure I could—"

"I am." Theresa bit her lip nervously. At Lynn's curious look, she explained hesitantly, "I have his social security number. I got it from a friend of a friend—a lab technician at the hospital where the insemination was done."

Lynn muttered a string of expletives beneath her breath. It wasn't like Theresa to be so reckless, usually she was cautious to the extreme. "Do you realize how close to the edge you are? You could be opening yourself up to blackmail or worse! What if this man finds out about you and Carter, likes what he sees and sues you for custody of his son?"

Theresa paled. Perspiration dotted her upper lip, her brow. "That won't happen, Lynn."

"How do you know?"

"Because I trust you to be able to protect Carter and me both."

"You're asking a lot."

"I know." She paused and took a deep, calming breath. "Look, if you can't do it, I understand." Abruptly, Theresa seemed close to tears again, although this time they were born of frustration.

"It isn't that I don't want to help." Lynn clasped both hands together, her fingers intertwined. She suddenly felt as jittery as if she were walking on a high wire a hundred feet above the ground with no safety net underneath her.

"You just can't do anything this crazy," Theresa said, guessing Lynn's thoughts. "I know," she repeated tiredly, "it's a risk."

"Yes, it is, to you more than others."

Theresa's expression tightened mutinously. "I'm doing it anyway."

Lynn could see she was determined. "Even if you have to go elsewhere to find your answers?" she asked softly.

She shrugged and pushed out of her chair. "We're friends, but you aren't the only private investigator in Indianapolis. I've already looked in the phone book, picked out a couple of names."

"Hold it right there." Lynn knew from her years as a police officer that more than half of the state's private detectives couldn't be trusted to *do* all the work they charged clients for, never mind keep secrets. What if Theresa hired someone inept, someone who got caught snooping around? All he or she would have to do was talk, and criminal charges, lawsuits and countersuits would follow. Lynn couldn't let that happen. Nor did she know anyone trustworthy enough to refer to Theresa.

That quickly, she made her decision. "Look, if you're really serious about this, I'll do it." She didn't want to do it, but on the other hand she couldn't throw

Theresa and her son to the wolves, and live with her conscience later.

"I promise you, I won't cause any trouble. I'll keep everything you tell me in strictest confidence. I just want to make sure Carter's health is protected, that I know everything there is to know in that regard."

With a sinking heart, Lynn studied her old friend. She hadn't even started the investigation and already she was loathing it and the unsettled way it made her feel. "You're sure you won't reconsider?" She really wished Theresa would.

"One way or another I'm determined to follow up on the donor's medical history."

"I won't give you a name, you know," Lynn cautioned. She would never reveal his identity to anyone.

"I don't want to know a name. Just the medical facts." Their conversation finished, she walked Lynn to the door. "Thanks, Lynn. You won't regret this."

Lynn sighed. She sincerely hoped not.

"SO YOU'RE GOING to be spending another day passing out agency flyers?" Lynn's brother Noland asked one week later.

Lynn nodded, buttering the toast. While her father scrambled eggs for the three of them, Noland poured orange juice and set the table. Lynn and Noland had moved back home with their dad after the breakup of their marriages because both were struggling financially. Noland was still making mortgage payments on his home that he was selling so he and his soon-to-be ex-wife could split the profits and move on. And Lynn had just started her own business and had very little cash flow at the moment. The arrangement, though unusual, worked for the three of them, and they made a point of having breakfast together daily and dinner whenever possible.

"Then I've got a business meeting late this afternoon," Lynn continued. She was meeting Theresa directly after work, to tell her all she had learned about Carter's father. "I'll probably be late coming in."

"How's the case you've been working on the past few days coming along?" Noland asked. No one but Lynn knew she was investigating or for whom, just that she'd been very preoccupied and unusually quiet.

"It's almost finished," she said.

"Hence the flyers," her father guessed. "Which means you need another case."

"And soon." Lynn sighed. "When I opened my own agency I had no idea it would be so hard to acquire clients."

"Give it time," Noland said. "It's been less than two months."

"Easy for you to say. Meanwhile, my salary has been cut in half."

"Temporarily," her father soothed. "It'll pick up."

"I hope so." Lynn sighed. In the meantime, she was leaving no possible source of employment unexplored. She had left flyers detailing her business, qualifications and fees at every attorney's office in the greater Indianapolis area. She also hit the schools, social services divisions, county courts and the various law enforcement agencies. Today, she was hitting every medical doctor in the area, as well as all the hospitals and clinics. By the time she finished, she figured there would be no one in all of Indianapolis who wouldn't have heard of the Lynn O'Brien Agency.

Four o'clock found her in the east wing of the University Medical Center. She was systematically going into every physician's office to hand out a flyer when she came to Dr. Jack Taggart's door. She paused in front of it, not wanting to go in. She didn't want to know any more about the man than she already did. She especially didn't want to know what he looked like, if he resembled Carter, or vice versa.

But if she were to skip his office when she'd already hit every other doctor's office in the entire center, wouldn't that arouse suspicion? Where was her professionalism? Like it or not, she might meet the man some other place, some other time, and she would have to behave as if he were an ordinary stranger to her, someone she hadn't investigated. There was no alternative—she had to go in and brazen it out, if for no other reason than to prevent anyone from wondering why she would skip Jack Taggart's office.

Figuring that if she hurried all she would be likely to meet would be his secretary, Lynn took a deep breath and opened the door. The reception area was empty. She was relieved to be able to simply leave the flyer on the reception desk. She turned to go and was almost to the front door when a man in rolled-up shirtsleeves and loosened tie came out into the waiting room. "Hi. What can I do for you?"

She'd didn't even have to ask. She knew from the dark hair and blue eyes that the man before her was Carter Richards's father. It was uncanny how he and Carter looked so much alike. Her heart started pounding, her hands perspiring. She wished she'd never ventured in there in the first place because this was exactly what she'd been afraid of.

Jack Taggart was looking at her curiously, taking in her nervousness.

Lynn forced herself to calm down. She gave him a too-bright smile, keeping her golden-brown eyes steady on his. "Hi. I'm Lynn O'Brien. I'm passing out flyers." Somehow, she managed to speak with the pleasant politeness she used with everyone.

Once she regained her equilibrium, he, too, relaxed slightly. He took the flyer she handed him and with interest, quickly scanned the printed information there. "You were a cop for twelve years?" His eyes met hers in a way that let her know he considered this part of her training of vital importance.

Unable to forget what she knew about him, she almost squirmed under his keen gaze. "Yes, I was," she said, keeping her tone light and affable with effort. Right now she wished she were back on the force.

He stared at her a moment, then gave her a straightforward, uncomplicated smile. Still unremittingly curious, he asked gently, "Why'd you quit?"

She felt herself beginning to relax despite her apprehension. It was clear Jack Taggart was in the right profession. This was a man who'd be very easy to confide in. "I was frustrated because I could never do enough for any particular case. The missing persons department is run according to some very strict rules.'' She couldn't help but notice how tall he was. Standing beside him, her mouth was level with his shoulder.

Taking a deep breath, she went on in a casual tone, aware now of an aching dryness in her throat. "Most of the rules are there for a reason. But when you have to tell a husband you can't look for his wife until twenty-four hours have passed, or deal with an understandably hysterical mother whose teenager has just run away for the third time with the car, a cache of drugs, no driver's license and all the family's credit cards, it's not so easy to live by those rules. So I quit, hoping that by becoming a private investigator I could devote myself to my cases in ways I was never able to when I was on the force."

Respect glimmered in his blue eyes. "In that case, I'm very glad you stopped by, Lynn. I'm Jack Taggart." He held out his hand.

Lynn reluctantly returned the handclasp. Darn it all anyway, why did he have to be so personable? Why did he have to understand her? And why did she suddenly have the feeling she was walking on hot coals just being near him, and that he'd noticed every single thing about her including the fact that she wore no wedding or engagement ring? "I really didn't expect to talk to you today," she said inanely, needing to think about something else besides how attractive he was, how tall and nice and ruggedly handsome.

"It's my afternoon off. I was doing paperwork."

"Oh. Well, don't let me interrupt." Finally, the excuse that would win her freedom.

She started to back away, but he held onto her hand, keeping her near. He studied her quietly, undoubtedly feeling the chill of her skin, the way she had started ever so slightly to tremble when he refused to immediately release his grasp on her. "Something's wrong," he said softly, never taking his eyes from hers. Suddenly she knew what it was like to be looked at under a microscope; he was that observant.

"Don't tell me," he said wryly, finally ending the slightly prolonged handshake, "you have a thing about psychiatrists, too."

"No. Not at all," she said truthfully. His profession didn't bother her. Knowing he had donated the sperm that created Carter Richards did. It was tough seeing him in person, after all her efforts not to. Now, she knew she would never forget him. It wasn't just that he was perceptive and attractive. There was something about him that went far beyond the high cheekbones and the sensual mouth, the slash of dark brows and smooth, lightly tanned skin. It was a chemistry, the feeling that she wanted to know more about this man—in every respect. But she couldn't, she didn't dare get close to him. For her sake, for Theresa's, for Carter's, for his.

Jack continued soothingly. "You don't have to be embarrassed, Lynn. I understand. Believe me, it happens all the time. People discover what I do for a living, or really think about it, and suddenly all they want to do is hide from me." He paused. "Although

I wouldn't have expected it from a private investigator. Surely, in your line of work, you've—"

"I've spoken to a psychiatrist or two," Lynn affirmed dryly. *Just not Carter Richards's father.* She put a hand to her forehead, feigning reason for her strange behavior. She had to do something to throw him off the trail. "It's not your profession. It's just I'm feeling a little funny, that's all. I've been passing our flyers since nine this morning without a break and—"

"No lunch!"

"None," Lynn answered truthfully. She'd been so busy she'd forgotten, but then she rarely had lunch and breakfast both in one day.

"The medical center has a great cafeteria. I'd be glad to walk you down there."

She couldn't miss the interested gleam in his eyes. A relationship with him, she didn't need. Theresa's case, and Lynn's part in it, was complicated enough as it was. She couldn't add fraternizing with the unsuspecting father to the mess.

Lynn smiled. "Thanks, but I've got a meeting across town in an hour, so I'd—" Despite her efforts to stay unaffected, his warm gaze had sent a blush to her cheeks.

"No time for even a cup of coffee, hmm?" he asked, smiling persuasively at her. "I'd really like to hear more about your work."

He was serious in his interest. Unfortunately she couldn't afford to encourage even that. "Thank you, no, not today," she declined his invitation pleasantly, wanting only to get out of there fast. It was all she could do not to fidget restlessly and give herself away.

"Sometime soon then?" Jack asked, watching her steadily.

She backed toward the door. "I don't know. I—I'll have to see." Her hand touched the doorknob and her knees weakened slightly. "I've really got to go now."

To her relief, he made no further attempt to stop or divert her. As she made her escape down the hall, she told herself it was for the best but even as she did so, she felt a little depression cloud her senses. Under any other circumstances he would have been a man worth meeting, a man she would have wanted to get to know better.

An hour later, Lynn was with Theresa as scheduled, dutifully filling her in on the facts about Carter's biological father. "He's a professional person, well educated. As far as I could discover he has no health problems." He'd certainly looked healthy enough!

"Then I don't have to worry about Carter on that score." Theresa closed her eyes briefly. "Lynn, you don't know how much better this has made me feel," she said, breathing a sigh of relief.

Unfortunately, Lynn felt ten times worse. Because she had now met Jack Taggart, talked to him and liked him, too. Worse, he was in his mid-thirties, single, and definitely interested in her. But would he feel that way if he knew of her investigation, if he knew he had an adorable four-year-old son?

"He doesn't know anything?" Theresa asked, a worried expression on her face.

"No. I didn't tell anyone I was conducting an investigation for you." She'd gotten her facts about Jack from a variety of sources, but no one had a clue as to why she had wanted to know all that she did.

"Oh, thank goodness. If anyone tried to take Carter away from me, I don't know what I'd do."

"That's not going to happen, Theresa."

"I hope not," Theresa was quiet. "Since this whole thing started, I've felt like I was in the middle of a nightmare."

Lynn had figured Theresa would feel that way sooner or later and was glad she was coming to her senses so swiftly, before any real damage had been done. "Regrets?"

Theresa's expression was troubled. "Yes. More than I knew that it was possible to have. But I had to do it because I want to do everything possible to protect Carter's health."

"I can understand that."

Theresa changed the subject abruptly. "Did I tell you I've decided to look into finding him a Big Brother to take his mind off his daddy?"

Lynn smiled. "I'm sure Carter will enjoy that."

"Yes, I know he will." Theresa hugged Lynn impulsively. "Listen, thanks for being such a good friend."

"That's what I'm here for," Lynn said lightly, glossing over the emotional turmoil she had suffered in the course of her investigation.

"To handle 'delicate family matters,'" Theresa quoted from Lynn's flyer.

"Right." Lynn didn't like knowing Jack was the biological father, but like any other confidential information she learned in the course of her work, the information had to be filed away and forgotten. It was part of her ethical obligation to her clients, similar to the professional obligations doctors and lawyers showed their patients.

She couldn't help but think, though, that it would have been much easier for her to do this if she hadn't met Jack at all.

LYNN RETURNED HOME that evening exhausted and emotionally wrung out, only to find her brother was having an even worse time of it. "Gail called me today," he admitted wearily, looking suddenly drained and unhappy. He lifted his golden-brown eyes to hers. "She said the date for our final divorce hearing has been set."

"When is it?" Lynn asked, knowing this shouldn't have been any surprise to her. Noland and Gail had separated off and on for over two years now because she couldn't handle the stress of being a cop's wife, and he, the son of a devoted cop, refused to give up the high-pressure, high-risk life.

"November first." Noland looked unbearably sad. His broad shoulders slumped. With effort, he shook off his low mood and went over to stir up the fire in the fireplace. "But enough about that."

Lynn and her dad exchanged worried glances. Both had hoped Noland and Gail would reconcile.

Determined to change the subject, Noland asked Lynn, "How's your new computer working out?"

It was Lynn's turn to groan. They'd hit on a subject she loathed to discuss. "So far the machine I bought to save me time has done nothing but cost me time."

Her father looked up from his newspaper. Although his golden hair had long ago turned white, his face was unlined, his eyes were bright and probing. He was nearing retirement age, but he didn't look or act it. "That's because you didn't study your manual," he said bluntly.

Lynn blushed. Leave it to her father to pick up on her deliberate omission.

"If you were smart, Lynn, you'd not even use that computer of yours until you understood and knew how to use every function!" he added.

"That would take years!" Lynn grumbled. As it was, she'd already spent far too much time—nearly two weeks—getting comfortable with the darn machine.

Noland grinned, still teasing her relentlessly, "And we all know that's far too long for Lynn." He winked at his dad. "Remember the time she decided to assemble that porch swing without looking at the directions once?"

They all laughed, even Lynn, though the joke was on her. When the phone rang, she went to answer it, glad for the reprieve. As she picked up the receiver,

Noland and her Dad were debating whether the blindly assembled swing had looked more like one half of a very strange picnic table or a post-modern sculpture.

"Hello."

"Lynn? This is Jack Taggart."

The sound of his voice sent warmth rushing through her veins. "Hi," she said cautiously, after a moment. Needing to concentrate, she turned her back to the men. They quieted down, their voices lowering to a barely discernible murmur in the background.

"I've done some checking. You've got an excellent reputation in the community," Jack said.

"Thanks." She knew it was silly and irrelevant, but she was glad he knew she was well thought of.

"I'd like to talk to you about a potential client, an uncle of mine. Would it be possible for us to get together tomorrow, maybe have lunch?"

Lynn paused. She'd never before worked with anyone she'd also secretly investigated. It wouldn't be wise to start now. On the other hand, she needed every job she could get. And this case involved someone other than Jack himself. He was just the go-between, and after this initial meeting, she was sure she'd never have to see him again. She was a professional, she could handle one more encounter; for her fledgling business, she would do so. "Sure," she said finally, unable to keep the smile out of her voice. "Just name the time and place."

Chapter Two

"Thank you for coming," Jack said, looking across the table at Lynn.

"How could I turn down a job?" She smiled but would not meet his gaze. Instead, she inspected the restaurant, which was crowded with business people.

He had wanted to see her, he admitted to himself, not so much for his uncle's sake but for his. He hadn't been able to stop thinking about her since they'd met. He wasn't sure why she'd made such an impression on him; after all, he'd met his share of women over the years. He just knew he hadn't been able to get her out of his mind. There'd been something about her, perhaps it was the slightly nervous way she'd dealt with him in his office, that nagged at him even now.

On a strictly physical level, it wasn't odd that he'd find her hard to forget. With her striking combination of golden-brown eyes and wavy, shoulder-length golden-brown hair, she would have made any man sit up and take notice. Tall and slim, she was wearing a stylish, nut-brown tweed blazer, baggy pleated trousers and a V-necked, cream-colored satin shirt that complemented the pale creaminess of her skin and the flush on her cheeks. On the surface, she looked fully in control of her self and the world around her. Yet today as in the previous afternoon, she seemed unnerved and on edge, which was very peculiar for a woman who was confident enough of her abilities that she had her own private detective agency. Was her take-charge appearance simply deceptive, he wondered, or was it something more? Perhaps she was expecting him to put the moves on her—an assumption not too far removed from the truth—and wasn't sure how to reject his advances without losing his case referral. Asking her for a date was very much in his mind, but he also didn't want to do anything that would make her uncomfortable. Maybe it would help if he concentrated on taking it nice and slow.

"So you wanted to talk to me about your uncle," Lynn said after the waiter had taken their orders.

Jack nodded. "His name is Walter Ohlendorf. He needs some investigative work done."

Lynn spread her napkin across her lap. Now that they were talking business, she seemed perfectly at ease. "Is there some reason why Mr. Ohlendorf chose not to contact me himself?"

Jack rested his forearms on the table on either side of his plate. He had to choose his words carefully so as not to put her off. There was a good reason why Uncle Walter hadn't approached her directly—Jack had asked him not to. He'd wanted the excuse to see her again.

"It's a very sticky situation, so I wanted to talk to you first," he said finally. She was watching him steadily, no expression readily apparent on her face. "Uncle Walter's a great guy, but he's also been through a very rough couple of years recently. He's retired, and his wife died unexpectedly the year before last. So now he's got too much time and a lot of money on his hands."

"Is he in any trouble?" Lynn asked gently.

"No, not just yet. It's what he wants to do in the future that's the problem. He wants to buy into a development project, a sort of resort for senior citizens. A bunch of retired folks, including Sheila, this new lady friend of his, are going in on it. He's told me a little bit about it, and it sounded like a risky deal. So I convinced him to get someone to look into it before he actually signed on the dotted line."

Lynn's brows drew together. "I take it he wants everything done quietly."

"Right. In case the whole thing's perfectly legitimate. He doesn't want to embarrass anyone needlessly.

Their waiter came back with their lunches—chef's salad and iced tea for both. As soon as he left, Lynn asked, "Is your uncle the kind of person who's easily taken in?"

Jack picked up his fork. "Well, to tell the truth, since my aunt died, he's been overdoing it a bit, playing it fast and loose. But as he says all the time, he's never going to get a chance to sow wild oats if he doesn't do it now since he didn't do it in his youth."

Lynn grinned, imagining an old man running around in such a way that had his nephew worried. "He sounds like quite a character."

"Yeah, he's that, all right. But he's pretty vulnerable whether he realizes it or not. I don't want to see anybody taking advantage of him." He sounded very definite about that.

"If this scheme turns out to be not on the up and up, it might get dangerous," she said, feeling compelled to caution him.

But he didn't look shocked at this prediction. Instead he smiled and said, "I'm sure you've faced similar situations before and can handle yourself."

She hadn't meant for him to take her statement as concern for herself, but she was too taken aback at the unexpected compliment to correct him.

"You'll take the case?" he asked.

She nodded. "I'll need your uncle's phone number."

He wrote it down on a piece of paper and handed it to her. Their fingers touched momentarily, sending prickles of warmth throughout her arm. She looked up to his eyes, and their gazes locked.

She was the first to look away, as Jack had expected. Abruptly, she acted as if she wanted to be anywhere else in the world except in the same room with him. She glanced at her watch, expressing great surprise that nearly an hour had passed. "Gosh. I had no idea we'd been here so long," she lamented. "I've really got to be going."

She's running again, Jack thought. *She's running from me. Why? What have I done?* he wondered. "You're sure you don't want to stay and have coffee or dessert?" He had to get back to the office, too, but he found himself wanting to linger. They needed to spend time with each other to get to the point where she wouldn't behave so skittishly around him, as if she were afraid to be alone with him even for one second.

"No, I can't." Pulling her keys out from her purse, she smiled politely. "I've got a busy day ahead of me."

"Cases to solve," Jack quipped, holding her gaze once again.

For a long time, she couldn't look away. "Yes," she said finally, lowering her glance. "As a matter of fact, I'm meeting some other new clients in a few minutes." She stood up, then as an afterthought, added, "And thanks for the business. I really appreciate it."

"Anytime," Jack replied, feeling more intrigued with her than ever.

LYNN COULDN'T GET OUT of the restaurant fast enough. The whole time she'd been in there she'd felt flushed and ill at ease. And Jack had noticed it, she was sure. She supposed, he being a psychiatrist, there was no way he could avoid it. He probably interpreted body language as quickly and effortlessly as a teacher caught spelling errors on compositions. And her body language must have said she was hiding something.

As she walked to her car, she felt a great sense of frustration about her unexpected lack of professionalism. Why was she letting the situation get to her? It wasn't as if this was the first time she harbored confidential information about another person. During all her years on the police force she'd handled one delicate matter after another without blinking an eye. She'd never lost her composure. But now it was suddenly much harder for her to do. No matter how hard she tried, she couldn't get Jack Taggart off her mind and the fact that he was Carter Richards's father.

So she continued to feel guilty and on edge around Jack. Why couldn't she just file that knowledge away and go on with her life? Why couldn't she forget Jack's face, or the intense way he looked at her? He was such a gentleman and very attractive... and very interested in her. But to protect Theresa, Carter and herself she had to stay away from him as much and as far away as possible. He was too clever, too observant, and she was too vulnerable. Yet why even now did she find herself flirting with the hope of somehow, somewhere seeing him again?

With her mind still full of thoughts about Jack, she got into her car and drove to her next appointment.

WEALTHY AND SOCIALLY PROMINENT, the Montgomerys were deeply concerned about their only child. "We want you to find our twenty-one-year-old daughter Jessica." Alan Montgomery explained succinctly. "She ran away six weeks ago."

"And you haven't heard from her since?" Lynn frowned. Six weeks was a long time; whatever trail their daughter had left would be as cold as ice now.

"No, we haven't," he replied. He was tall and thin, very distinguished looking, while his wife, Mary, was plump and small, with fluttery hands and a nervous, somewhat timid disposition. They exchanged a troubled glance. "There was just that short note—saying she's going away to think and not to worry—that her roommate found on Jessica's bed the morning she disappeared."

"Why did she leave?" Lynn asked. She knew the question was rude and intrusive, but it was her job to get as much information as possible from them, and the sooner the better. They'd already wasted far too much time merely hoping Jessica would come home on her own.

Mary paled and looked down at her tightly clasped hands. "She left because we disapproved of her beau."

"What my wife means to say is we broke them up. And I'm still convinced we acted in Jessie's best interest."

Mary was silent, agreeing.

They went on to tell Lynn they wanted the search kept quiet. Understanding, she agreed to be discreet. Then Mary showed her countless photos of their daughter, who was beautiful and vivacious looking but also self-possessed and hence, capable of taking care of herself.

They talked some more and Lynn learned, among other things, that Jessica had emptied her bank account of slightly less than one thousand dollars the day before she disappeared, that she was a very bright girl but had no employable skills and was a C student in college, a business major who had yet to graduate.

"She knew I was grooming her to take over the family business." Alan frowned.

"She never was very interested in the Montgomery Corporation, though. And I don't think she enjoyed her business classes at all," Mary pointed out.

"Was she in good health?"

"Why, yes." Mary looked surprised by the question. "She was fine. With the exception of that doctor she was seeing." Mary bit her lip and glanced at her husband. He was frowning again.

Lynn knew she was on to something. "What doctor?" she asked gently.

Mary shot another look at her husband, then said finally, "That psychiatrist. Dr. Taggart."

"Jack Taggart?" Lynn asked, amazed.

"Yes, do you know him?" Mary asked.

Lynn nodded reluctantly, reeling from the shock of hearing his name again. So much for her decision to stay away from him. "Just slightly," she replied. "Why was Jessica seeing Dr. Taggart?"

"We don't know," Alan said bluntly. "We only found out about it after she left when an unpaid bill was forwarded from her sorority house to us."

"Did you speak to Dr. Taggart about Jessica?"

"Oh, yes. He knows she ran away," Alan said bitterly. "And it makes absolutely no difference to him. He still won't tell us why she was seeing him. Patient-doctor confidentiality."

Lynn sighed. "Well, Jessica is twenty-one."

"That doesn't mean she's old enough to know what she's doing." Alan scowled.

Lynn was beginning to see why Jessica might have found it necessary to run away. Her parents meant well, but they were a little overprotective.

Feeling she'd gotten all the information she could that night, she gathered up her notes and several recent photos of Jessica. "I'll get started on this right away," she promised.

"Will you do us a favor?" Mary asked, as she walked Lynn to the door. "Would you go and see Dr. Taggart, explain the situation to him? See if maybe *you* can't get him to help us or at least give us a clue as to where Jessica might have gone?"

"What makes you think Dr. Taggart would know where she is?" Lynn asked.

Mary smiled tremulously. "Because he was one of the last people to see Jessica before she left town. If Jessie had told anyone, I think she would have confided in him."

FACE IT, Jack Taggart is not going to want to see you about this, Lynn thought as she guided her car out of the Montgomerys' driveway. But she'd just promised Mrs. Montgomery she would question Jack about his former patient, so she had to try, at least.

First she had to decide when and where to approach him. His office was the logical place, but it was also the worst. In a clinical setting, he was most likely to refuse to cooperate. Whereas in a casual setting, he'd be most relaxed, perhaps more apt to cooperate.

She glanced at her watch, noting it was just after five-thirty. She wondered whether he was home by now. Maybe the thing to do was simply drop by his house, get invited in, then gently hit him with what she wanted to know. It might make him angry, being approached that way, but under the circumstances it was the best plan she could come up with. Besides, he'd probably be irritated with her anyway. To ask him anything about Jessica would be to put him on the spot. On the other hand, he was probably as concerned as her parents were about the young woman's welfare and wanted her happy and safe, also. She would simply have to make Jack understand that she, too, was working only in Jessica's best interest.

Fortunately, luck was with her. Jack was home and answered the door promptly. Surprise was evident on his face.

Lynn gave him no chance to say anything. She gave him her most engaging smile. "Hi. I hope you don't mind my dropping by on the spur of the moment."

He smiled back at her, looking perplexed but glad to see her nonetheless. "No, of course not," he said softly. "I am a little curious, though...how did you know where I live?"

How did she know where he lived? She'd just concluded an investigation of him that was how. She remembered belatedly that his home address was not in the phone book; she had gotten it off his driver's license via the police department. Purposefully making light of the situation, Lynn said, "I'm a private detective, remember?"

As she had hoped, Jack looked amused by her flirtatious response and didn't press her further, chalking it up, she supposed, to feminine wiles and a need to be a tad mysterious.

"Right." He stepped aside to let her pass.

The inside of his condominium was impressively neat. Bookshelves flanked both sides of the fireplace. Two emerald-green sofas formed a conversation area. An antique wood-and-leather trunk served as a coffee table. There was a state-of-the-art stereo and television, as well as a much-used rolltop desk. The mixture was eclectic and very much like him; it was obvious he'd chosen each piece with care.

He motioned for her to sit down. "So what brings you here? Surely you don't already have news to give about my uncle's case. Or am I mistaken?"

Simultaneously she felt relieved he was alone and anxious, as if she had just stepped into the lion's den. It was altogether too cozy there, she noted.

"Uh, it's about a different business, actually. I have a favor to ask you."

His smile widened, as if he wanted nothing more than to be able to do something for her.

Lynn took a deep breath and plunged on heedlessly, "I've just started working on a case for the Montgomery family."

His welcoming look faded. He looked wary and stiff, about as movable as the Rocky Mountains. "And they want information about their daughter, I suppose?" There was a decided edge to his voice.

Boy, had she hit a sore spot. Lynn had to fight to keep her face expressionless. "Yes," she nodded, forcing herself to maintain an encouraging manner, no matter how discouraged she felt.

"Forget it." He stood abruptly. He rubbed at the muscles between his shoulders. "I've already told them all that I can."

If Jack had been as uncooperative with the Montgomerys as he was with her, they had reason to be irritated with him, Lynn thought. Didn't he understand what Jessica's family was going through? Or was he more concerned with protecting his patient, than anything her parents might be going through?

"Forget what you know from your dealings with Jessica professionally," Lynn advised easily, staying right where she was, although she knew from Jack's stony expression that he wished she would leave right at that moment. "Do you think this could be an elopement? Is it possible the Montgomerys didn't really break up Jessica and her beau?" She was fishing. She wanted only to get him talking, to tell her something, anything, even in anger. "What was her state of mind when she left town? The Montgomerys assert you were one of the last people here in Indianapolis to see her."

Jack exhaled slowly, as if he was mentally counting to ten. He took three strides toward her and didn't look like a man to be toyed with. "Look," he said between lightly clenched teeth, "as much as I'd like to help Jessica's family, I can't. It's a matter of patient-doctor confidentiality. Beyond that, there's nothing in my files that would indicate where she's run off to. I have no idea where she is. I didn't even know she was leaving.''

"The Montgomerys are very worried about their daughter,'' she reminded him patiently.

His gaze held hers deliberately, and she felt her pulse begin to race. "I know that and I'm sorry.'' His concern for the Montgomerys plight was genuine, but he wasn't backing down from his decision to remain mute about why Jessica was seeing him.

"That's it? You're sorry?'' She was baiting him again—deliberately—hoping to goad him into revealing something.

He took another two steps toward her, obliterating what little space there had been between them. He stood, towering over her chair, and the look on his face was anything but patient. "There's been no evidence of foul play. Nor has Jessica herself asked me to talk to you. In fact, under the circumstances of her running away, I'm sure she'd be strongly against it.''

Lynn studied him wordlessly. It was clear it was time to give up; Jack wouldn't tell her anything. And that made her angry. She hated it when people withheld information that could help locate a missing person. She stood up and prepared to leave, trying one last time to reason with Jack. "One of the things I learned when I was on the police force is that the more time elapses after a person disappears the more difficult it is to trace them. I sincerely believe the Montgomerys love their daughter and that whatever problems the three of them have can be worked out. I'm only asking you to help.''

''I told you,'' he repeated tiredly, an unsympathetic light in his eyes, ''I've already told them everything I can. There's nothing more I can add to that.''

''What you mean is you won't help,'' Lynn corrected icily, as she headed unescorted toward his front door. Talking to him on this subject was like talking to a stone.

He didn't differ with her, merely stood silently and watched her go.

Damn, she thought. It was difficult enough before, knowing what she did about Jack and Carter, but now the man was not only going to be an all-too-potent reminder of the sticky paternity case she unwillingly investigated but also a major block in her path to solving the Montgomery case as well. If she believed in fate, she'd almost think she and Jack were destined to keep crossing paths.

Chapter Three

"I expected you to change your mind about having me investigate for your uncle," Lynn said later that evening when Jack picked her up at her house. She'd come home from his place to find a message from him on her office answering machine, saying his uncle had called. Walter had insisted on meeting her right away, and had ordered Jack to bring her to the club where he was dining that evening with Sheila.

The arrangement was unorthodox, but from the little she knew of Walter, Lynn guessed that wasn't too far off for him. And she wasn't about to back out on much-needed work. Besides, she wanted to get back on Jack's good side since she was sure he knew something that would help her with the Montgomery case. Also, deep down, no matter how much she didn't want to admit it, she relished the thought of seeing him yet again.

She had dressed with more than her usual care, choosing a long-sleeved and high-necked dress that fell above her knees. She knew the simple garment made her look competent, yet somehow feminine, too.

"I thought about it, believe me," he said, his hands thrust deep in his pockets.

"Why didn't you?" Lynn stopped walking. If he was still upset, it would be better if they cleared the air now.

He turned to face her. "Because I realized that your tenacity and intrusiveness are what's needed for Uncle Walter's case, and that my feelings shouldn't jeopardize a successful investigation of it. Which means that tonight I'm trying to keep your work for the Montgomerys completely out of my mind."

In other words, he was here because she had a job to do. "Truce?" She offered her hand.

He took it, and she felt his warm, smooth fingers surround hers. "Truce," he said softly.

They got in his car, and he seemed so close to her that she had to talk about something to dispel the tension surrounding them. "Tell me more about Uncle Walter. You're pretty close to him, aren't you?"

"Yeah, I am." Jack nodded, trying hard not to notice how her silky, perfumed presence filled his car. "He was always there for me when I was a kid."

"More so than your own parents?"

"Not my mom, but my dad, yeah." He sighed, searching for the right words. "My dad was an attorney specializing in labor relations. He's a very caring man, but his job demanded he be gone frequently from home. So when I was growing up, I didn't see him a lot. On the other hand, Uncle Walter, who's my mom's brother, lived right in the same town. He and my aunt were childless, and he seemed to have always been around. He was the one who helped me learn how to handle a ball and bat before I tried out for Little League. He was the one who helped me build a windmill in his basement workshop for the science fair. And yet he never forgot that he was my uncle, not my dad, so I never felt guilty about being very close to him.

Lynn leaned back in her seat. "How'd your dad feel about him?"

"He was glad that Uncle Walter was there when he couldn't be. He never resented that."

"Do your parents live around here?"

"No, they retired to Arizona about five years ago. Mom's arthritis was giving her a lot of trouble. The doctors felt living in a warm, dry climate would help her, and it has."

"Do you see them a lot?"

"Whenever I can, usually on holidays, and they fly up once every summer to visit me. What about you? Are you close to your folks?"

"You could certainly say that. I live with my father and my brother in the house I grew up in."

"And your mom?"

"She died when I was fifteen. Car accident."

"I'm sorry."

She nodded, her expression revealing for a moment the pain she'd felt at the loss.

He guided the car into the club parking lot, shut off the ignition, then turned to face her. "There's something I need to tell you about Uncle Walter," he began. "You see, he wants nothing more than to see me, his only nephew, married and become father to several children.''

Lynn raised her eyebrows, not sure where this was leading to. She felt a sudden pinprick of guilt—how would Uncle Walter react if he found out that Jack already had an adorable four-year-old son?

''So he's taken to matchmaking for me and likes to think I'm serious about every girl I introduce to him,'' he continued.

Feeling the need to compensate for the sudden upsurge of her conscience, lest she start acting on edge again, Lynn smiled a roguish smile. Her eyes glinting wickedly, she demanded, ''Just how many women have you been serious about?''

He squinted, thinking. ''Four, I guess.''

She opened her mouth to say she was only teasing and hadn't expected an answer, then decided that would be a mistake. To say anything might make him think she cared about his love life.

''Let's see,'' he said, apparently intent on giving her details. ''There was the first girl I ever dated, my high-school sweetheart, my college sweetheart, and my first wife. There's been no one recently, not since my divorce a couple of years ago.''

So they had that in common, she thought, then wondered why he had gotten divorced and if it had been at his instigation or his wife's.

''Anyway, Uncle Walter might start making suggestions about us. Just ignore them and don't let them throw you off,'' he advised.

Lynn nodded, although for one crazy moment she was tempted to say that she wouldn't mind getting a chance to get "serious" with him.

They got out of the car and walked toward the building. "Oh, one other thing," Jack said. "Uncle Walter would prefer you didn't talk about the investigation in front of Sheila. He mentioned it to her once, and she raved on about suspicious minds."

"Your uncle has a perfect right to check out the project before investing in it, no matter what anyone says."

"That's what I told him, but he doesn't want to have to fight with her about it."

"He's the boss," Lynn replied. Then after some thought, she asked, "We won't have to, uh, make up some story about me, do we?"

"What for? There's no reason we can't tell the truth—that we met while you were passing out flyers for your detective agency and that we just haven't been able to stay away from each other." He smiled. "And now you're meeting Uncle Walter because he wants to meet you. As he does all the women I'm interested in." He shot her a look and Lynn had to fight to keep her composure.

"You don't think she'll get suspicious about my being a P.I.?"

"If she does, that's something we can't help."

Lynn felt relieved. She had employed a little skulduggery before to get the job done, but only when absolutely necessary. It was great to work on a case where she didn't have to do that.

They went in and quickly found Walter's table. He turned out to be a very affable man, a bit overweight with dark gray hair that was thinning at the front and crown. To Lynn, he seemed the kind of man who was equally adept at bandaging a child's scraped knee and reading a complicated annual business report. Sheila was equally charming. In her sixties, she had black hair streaked liberally with gray, a soft voice and pleasant manner. It was very easy to see why Walter was taken with her.

"Jack tells me you're retired," Lynn said to Walter after they had exhausted the subject of her unusual line of work.

"Retired but not forgotten." Walter grinned. "Although I'm not busy enough. That's why I'm looking around for something to get involved in. And I think I found it, too." He eyed Jack carefully, then reached over to squeeze Sheila's hand. "Sheila and I are thinking of getting in on a resort upstate, kind of a Club Med for senior citizens. The Golden Glow resort is going to have everything—permanent residences for those who desire them, a hotel for those who want to stay just a short time, all sorts of recreational facilities and things to do...." His blue eyes glimmered as he continued to describe the paradise that Golden Glow was going to be.

When Sheila excused herself to go to the ladies' room, Lynn took advantage of her absence to ask Walter for the names of the people involved in the resort, including the fifteen other potential backers. He promised to drop off the names in her office soon.

Sheila returned just as music was beginning to issue from the band on the small stage. Walter looked at her and said, "Sounds like they're playing our song, hon."

She adjusted the sweater around her shoulders and stood when he held out her chair. "I'd be happy to dance with you, Walter," she said as graciously as any Southern belle.

Walter cast a questioning look at Jack. "Well, kid? Are you just going to sit there all night like a bump on a log or are you going to ask your date to dance?"

Jack turned to face his date, too stubborn to let his confusion show. The male part of him wanted nothing better than to hold her slim body in his arms, but the thinking part of him knew better. If Lynn got jittery just from having lunch with him, how would she react to dancing? Already she was looking panicky. But then again, he thought ruthlessly, having pressure put on her would probably be the only way he'd ever have her close to him. "Well, shall we?" He stood and pulled out her chair.

Walter nodded approvingly, and he and Sheila moved off, their steps light and lively.

"Jack, I really—it's been a very long, grueling day," she murmured.

"So?" he asked softly, his desire showing in his eyes. "Lean on me. I'll hold you up."

"I have weak ankles."

His gaze drifted languidly down her body, skimming over the soft curves and taking in the long, slender legs. "They look very fine to me."

She looked flushed and hot, exactly the way he felt. "I guess I'm just looking for a way out," she whispered, her tone telling him she intended to find one. But his answering look told her there wouldn't be one, no matter how hard she tried.

"Why don't you want to dance with me?" he asked softly, sitting down. He took her hand and pressed his lips to the palm.

Every muscle in her body tightened, and her thighs turned liquid. "I don't dance with clients."

"I'm not a client. My uncle is."

Of course he was right; why had she said that? Why was it suddenly so hard for her to think? And why did she feel as if she were on trial here, as if he could see right into her soul and the secret she held? Dimly, she was aware that the song ended and was followed immediately by another. "You never said anything about dancing being part of my work."

Jack grinned. "What's the matter? Don't you dance on the first date?"

It was a joke, meant only to tease, but he saw her stiffen. "This isn't a date," she said firmly.

"You're telling me you're involved with someone?" He was startled at how possessive he felt about her.

"No." She looked away.

"Still hung up on whoever came before me?"

"No."

"Then what?"

She sighed. "I just can't see you. It's impossible."

She tried to pull her hand free from his grasp, but he wouldn't let her go. "Why? What's going on?" She had a scared, hunted look on her face.

She took a deep breath. "I'm sorry, Jack. It's getting too muddled."

"Is it because I won't help with Jessica?" he asked, his voice pleading for a direct answer.

Suddenly, she stood up. "I've got to go home," she said. "I've got an early day tomorrow."

Jack nodded, knowing he had pushed her far enough for one night. "All right," he said quietly.

She smiled, her relief evident. And he had to wonder again, what was she hiding?

AFTER A RESTLESS NIGHT, Lynn awoke early, determined to keep busy all day so she wouldn't have time to dwell on the confused state of her personal life. First on her agenda was the Montgomery case, and at eight-fifteen, she was waiting outside Jack's office door. One way or another she was going to solve the case without his assistance.

"Can I help you?" a pleasant-looking woman in her mid-thirties approached, keys in one hand, her lunch and handbag in another.

Lynn smiled. "I'm looking for Dr. Taggart's secretary."

A puzzled expression on her face, the woman paused mid-stride. "I'm Andrea Howard, Dr. Taggart's secretary. I don't believe we've met."

"We haven't." Lynn held out her hand, which Andrea shook. "I'm Lynn O'Brien, a private investigator. I'm working for the Montgomery family. It's a personal matter, highly confidential." She stressed the last two words, then glanced at the closed office door. If this was going to work at all, she had to get Andrea inside and ferret out everything possible before Jack arrived. She hoped he wouldn't show up for another fifteen or twenty minutes, which would give her plenty of time.

"Oh, of course. We'll go inside. Although I'm not sure what I can tell you." Andrea juggled her belongings and unlocked the door.

Moments later they were settled inside the office in a small crowded room that seemed to double as a staff lounge and file room. "So what is it you want to know?" Andrea asked, scooping coffee into a filter.

Briefly, Lynn explained about Jessica.

Andrea nodded slowly, her expression becoming wary. "Look, I can't give you anything confidential."

"I understand. I wouldn't ask you to do that. But I've already spoken with Jack—Dr. Taggart—and he knows that I'm on the case." He just didn't know she was talking to his secretary. Keeping her voice brisk and businesslike, she continued, "What we're looking for here is not anything from the files or their sessions, but simply your impression of her state of mind. How was Jessica feeling the last few times she was here? Did she seem depressed or listless? Was she overly buoyant—as if she was about to do something daring or impulsive? Did she seem troubled to you at all?"

"Hmm. That's a good question." She paused to measure water into the coffee maker and switched it on. "It was only when Jessica first started coming here that she did seem troubled. I remember she used to arrive early and then pace in the waiting room while she waited to see the doctor."

"This may seem off the wall to you," Lynn said slowly, "but was Jessica in love with Dr. Taggart? I know it's a terribly rude question, but it's not uncommon for women to fall in love with their doctors. And since Jessica was so young and feeling so vulnerable, and since Dr. Taggart was the last one to see her...."

"You didn't ask Dr. Taggart this, did you?" Andrea asked in an aggrieved tone. She was half-annoyed, half-intrigued.

"No, I— You know how men are. I wasn't sure Dr. Taggart would even have noticed." But there was no way Jessica could have missed noticing Jack, Lynn thought. He was simply too attractive a man.

"Well, it's possible. I know she thought very highly of him." Andrea paused. Woman to woman, she asked, "Do you think that's why Jessica ran away, because she was in love with Jack, and knew, well, because of the age difference and the fact that she was a patient that he would never...?"

Lynn shrugged, letting her confusion show. "I really don't know. I'm clutching at straws here, hoping that Jessica is in a sound frame of mind, not seriously ill or disturbed."

"Oh, I don't think she would ever harm herself. She just didn't seem like the type."

And Andrea probably knew which of Jack's patients had ever made attempts to take their own lives. Knowing her time—and luck—was almost up, Lynn limited herself to one more question. "Do you think she was capable of taking care of herself? I've heard Dr. Taggart's opinion—" *sort of, anyway* "—and her parents, but I'd like to get your impression as well."

Because if Jessica was capable, it would be very difficult to find her unless she wanted to be found. And maybe she didn't want to be found.

"Oh, yes. Jessica could take care of herself," Andrea smiled. "And then some."

LYNN SPENT THE REST of the morning talking to two close friends of Jessica, all to no avail. They had not heard from her and had no clues as to why she had left town so suddenly and mysteriously. Early that afternoon, Lynn took a commuter flight to Cincinnati and drove to the firm where Jessica's ex-fiancé, Mario Marchetti, was now employed as a computer programmer. Although he too hadn't heard from Jessica, he volunteered to talk about her. He left work early, and they walked to a nearby coffee shop.

It was easy for Lynn to see why Jessica had been attracted to Mario. He was personable, bright, good-looking. Unfortunately, his olive complexion and dark hair had been unacceptable to the Montgomerys.

Lynn found this racism unforgivable, but Mario seemed to have taken it in stride. He looked straight at Lynn. "I wanted the best for Jessie," he said quietly. "I still do. It just wasn't and never will be me."

"Did she feel that way?" Lynn asked.

He shrugged and looked away, an expression of pain crossing his face. His voice husky, he continued, "Jessie always had these *West Side Story* ideas about us. Real romantic. The reality is—" he took a deep breath "—we were worlds apart and we always would be."

"I see." Lynn sighed.

"I already have another girlfriend," Mario seemed embarrassed to admit this. "A couple of days before you said she left she ran into us at an old hangout. It was a pretty bad scene."

Lynn could imagine. She knew how it felt to have a serious romantic relationship end. She knew how it felt to let the last of her romantic idealism go and take that first step toward growing up and facing the imperfection of the real world.

When she was twenty-one she was just as hopelessly romantic as Jessica. She fell in love with a boy she'd known since she was sixteen and despite her father's protestations, married him before the end of her second year at the community college. Robert was a business major, interested in having a family and building his own business. She wanted a family, too, but she also wanted a career on the police force. Robert understood that, and was proud of her goals initially, if only because he was the only guy he knew whose wife was a cop. But looking back on it she could see he had never been completely comfortable with the fact that his wife was a cop, that she carried a gun and often dealt with the scum of the earth, while he carried a briefcase and dealt with the cream of the crop. He would have been much happier with a well-dressed yuppie who had a nice, safe office job like his, or better yet, a woman who was content to stay home and bake bread and hang curtains.

They both knew when it was over, and that knowledge hadn't been easy to live with. She wanted to run away many times, but she didn't because she knew even then that running never solved anything.

"Tell Jessie I—" Mario stopped and swore. For long moments he'd been lost in thought, too, wrapped up in his own regrets and wishes. He shook his head, changing his mind about whatever he'd been about to say. "Scratch that," he said, turning a dull shade of red again. "Don't tell her anything."

Lynn studied him silently, seeing both pain and acceptance on his face. "It really is over, isn't it?" she asked softly.

Mario nodded. "Our romance was just one of those things that was never meant to be. And no amount of wishing on either of our parts could ever make it work out any different."

MARIO'S WORDS STAYED with Lynn on the way back to Indianapolis. By the time she pulled into her own driveway, it was eight forty-five. Lynn was exhausted, hungry and no closer to solving the Montgomery case than she had been at eight that morning.

So much for legwork, she thought, sighing and getting out of the car. But at least she was working.

"About time you got home," a low masculine voice growled from across the street. This was followed by the emphatic slam of a car door.

Lynn turned in the direction of the sound and the all-too-familiar voice. Swallowing hard, she looked over to see Jack Taggart striding furiously toward her. She hadn't paid any attention to the sleek navy BMW parked across the street when she drove up, but it was obvious now that the car was his and he had been sitting there, waiting for her.

"Where the hell do you get off grilling my secretary?" he demanded.

Lynn's mood wasn't the best to begin with, and his disapproving attitude just added more gasoline to the fire. She found herself responding in kind. "There aren't any laws against talking to secretaries as far as I know. I imagine quite a lot of secretaries talk to—"

She gasped as he caught her up short and pulled her against him. She hadn't expected him to have such a temper.

"You knew you were invading my privacy and that of my patient." He gave her a little shake, then let her go.

Lynn stumbled backward, then righted herself as gracefully as possible. She could feel her chest rising and lowering with each frantic attempt to breathe but she tried to appear calm. "All right, so I pushed it to the limit. I'm sorry if I offended you or overstepped my bounds."

"Sorry? That'll be the day!"

He was right. She wasn't the least bit sorry. In fact she was pleased she had pulled it off so effortlessly, especially after he'd refused to help her. "It's not as if I didn't come to you first," she pointed out defiantly, her heart racing.

"You couldn't have left it at that?" He took a threatening step nearer.

"No, I couldn't have." Rather than back away, she stepped forward, too, so they were standing toe-to-toe, the top of her head just reaching his chin. She tilted her head back to see his face better, planted her feet slightly apart and put both hands on her hips. Her aggressive stance matched her mood to a T. "For all I know every second counts. Jessica could be trying to kill herself now, this very moment, as we speak."

"Don't be absurd," he snorted. "Jessica isn't about to kill herself."

Ha! She'd finally gotten him—however inadvertently—to tell her something! "Then she is of sound mind," Lynn crowed.

He shook his head, then walked away.

Satisfaction welled up deep inside her, along with the knowledge that she was very definitely playing with fire. "You know, it doesn't have to be this way," she said, lowering her voice and trying for another truce. "We don't have to be enemies. We could work together on finding Jessica, try to bring her home." Maybe then she'd have a chance of finding her.

He stopped short and turned to face her. "First of all," he began, "Jessica is of age. She can do whatever she wants. She doesn't need our permission or her parents'. She doesn't need anyone looking over her shoulder.''

"Then she is capable of fending for herself?" Lynn asked.

Jack was silent, refusing to answer. Slowly, he walked back toward her, each step deliberate and slightly menacing.

Lynn had to fight not to give in to the urge to run.

"Second," he said, his eyes pinning hers, "what you did today was unforgivable. You had no right to go into my office and manipulate my secretary into giving out confidential information."

On some level, Lynn knew that. But she also knew she had pledged to help the Montgomerys find their daughter, and Jack was the best lead she had. "Andrea didn't tell me anything she shouldn't have," she said softly, meaning it.

"She shouldn't have told you word one," Jack reiterated fiercely.

"You're not going to fire her, are you?" Lynn asked, aghast. If she had cost Andrea her job, Lynn would never forgive herself!

"No, I'm not going to fire her. I am warning you, though. I won't be a part of your unethical snooping. Nor will anyone in my office. So don't you ever, ever try that again. Got it?"

She knew he wanted her to ask forgiveness; she wouldn't do it. "Forewarned is forearmed," she said lightly, goading him with an insouciance she couldn't begin to feel.

He turned on his heel and stomped away. Lynn issued a sigh of profound relief, then waited until he'd gotten about five feet away before she interjected coolly, "Taggart, there's one thing you should know."

He pivoted slowly, daring her to go on.

She met and held his stormy gaze, refusing to waver. "Whether you help me or not, I will find Jessica."

Chapter Four

The phone rang in the middle of the night, jarring Jack out of a sound sleep. He reached for the phone, pulling it into bed with him. "'Lo," he mumbled groggily, trying to blink himself awake.

It was the operator asking if he'd accept charges for a collect call from Jessica. He said yes, thinking *Hallelujah*. Then there was a short silence, followed by Jessica's low, anxious voice.

"Dr. Taggart? I woke you, didn't I?"

"Don't worry about it." He sat up quickly, pulling the covers up around his waist. "What's going on?"

"I just needed to talk to someone."

"Everything okay?" Jack asked gently, wishing he could see her face to better assess her emotional and physical condition.

"Yes and no." Her voice was thick with unshed tears.

Easy now, you don't want to scare her. "Where are you, Jessica?"

Silence.

"Your parents are worried about you."

"They called you?" Hope flared in her voice.

"Several times," Jack admitted, wondering even as he spoke if this was a juvenile ploy for parental attention on Jessica's part. Somehow he didn't think so, though he knew from their sessions that she had never really gotten along with her folks, and that she was also pampered and spoiled and had been from the day she was born. Had it been anyone else, he'd have thought that the whole business of running away was just an act of willfulness, a grand tantrum. But he knew instinctively that with Jessica it wasn't that at all. But what, he couldn't figure out. "Have you talked to your folks?" he asked gently. "Called them to let them know you're all right, at least?"

"No!"

"Why not?" he asked gently.

"Because we'd just fight," Jessica admitted tiredly.

Was that what she was running from, the traditional parent-child conflict? Was this the only way she could cut the apron strings? Or was it something else, something deeper?

"I'm sorry I woke you, Dr. Taggart. I realize now I shouldn't have called."

"Jess—"

"I've got to go."

Click. She hung up.

Jack was left staring at the receiver in his hand, feeling a frustration deeper than any he'd ever known.

He spent the rest of the night tossing and turning. This wasn't his problem, not really, he instructed himself firmly. Jessica had told him at their last session that she was going away for a while, to travel, to think. Jack had not argued because he knew she wasn't ready to talk to him about whatever it was that was eating at her, but that when she was, she would come back. If not to him, then to some other psychiatrist. He hadn't realized she meant to run away. Still, as an adult, that had been her choice, even if he didn't approve of it. But this last call jarred his confidence in his judgment. What if he had missed something? What if something traumatic had happened to her since he last saw her that had prompted her to run away? What if she were really headed toward the edge? Could he live with himself if anything did happen to Jessica? Was Lynn right not to leave it alone, but to pull out all the stops to find try and find her?

"I'M GLAD YOU COULD FIND TIME to meet me on such short notice," Jack said, standing as Lynn approached his table and slid into the booth beside him. It was lunchtime, and the coffee shop was very busy.

"I gathered it was urgent." Lynn looked at him coldly and smiled nonchalantly.

Jack smiled back. He knew the only reason she had agreed to see him at all was because he'd told her he wanted to talk about Jessica.

He waited only long enough for the waiter to deliver two cups of coffee before asking, "How's the Montgomery case going?"

"About as well as can be expected," Lynn said bluntly and offered nothing more.

He stared at her in frustration, watching her stir cream into her coffee. "She hasn't contacted her parents?" he asked evenly.

"No. Why? Has she contacted you?" Lynn lifted the cup to her lips.

Looking at her and glancing beyond the surface hostility generated no doubt by their last passionate meeting, Jack saw an interest in her clients' child that was earnest and heartfelt. Maybe he shouldn't, but he had the feeling he could trust her, at least when it came to her commitment to find Jessica. And right now that was exactly what he needed, he decided, remembering the urgency of Jessica's phone call. "She called me last night," he confided finally.

Lynn put down her cup. "When?"

"About 2:00 a.m."

Lynn's brows lifted wonderingly, he could guess what she was thinking. "That's pretty late. Did she . . . make a habit of it?"

"No," Jack replied quietly, his steady, unrepentant gaze disabusing her of the notion that there had been anything at all going on between him and his patient. "In fact that's the first time she's called me at home," he stressed quietly.

Lynn looked skeptical. "How'd she get your number?"

"I give all my patients my home number—in case of a crisis." He read her doubts about the procedure and commented, "Very few of them ever abuse it. And it helps them to know they have someone they can count on."

"I see." She was silent, still watching him, a guarded expression on her face. "So what did Jessica say last night?"

Jack shrugged, wishing he had more to reveal. "Not much."

"But you're worried."

"Yes," he confessed finally, deciding he had to be straight with her if they were ever to find Jessica. "I am."

"Want to tell me why?"

No, he didn't. He didn't want to admit he felt he had failed Jessica in some way, that although she'd left his office feeling stronger, she hadn't ever completely revealed what had been on her mind in the first place. "I just want to know she's all right."

"So do we all," Lynn said softly, her eyes never leaving his face. Jack noticed the compassion in them and found his senses begin to stir.

"Did she say where she was calling from?"

"No."

Lynn leaned back, until her shoulders pressed against the high back of the wine-colored, padded leather booth. "Not a clue as to how you could reach her?"

"No."

Her lips pressed together in frustration. She brushed it aside with effort. "How'd she sound?"

Jack took a sip of his coffee and found it had cooled. "Upset, depressed, unsure of herself." That had bothered him more than he could say. Because the last time he'd seen her in his office she seemed as if she was well on the road to resolving her problems. Now it seemed as if she had backtracked.

Lynn removed a small notepad from her purse and pushing her coffee out of the way, began jotting down notes. "Was it a local call or long distance?" she asked, all business.

Jack started. He hadn't even thought of that. What a clue to overlook! "It was long distance."

Lynn made another notation. "Have you had the call traced?"

"No."

"Would you object if I did?"

Jack thought of Jessica. If she was in trouble...even though it went against everything he believed in... "No, I wouldn't mind."

"Good." She sighed her relief. Later, she'd ask one of her police friends to pay an "official" visit to the phone company. She smiled with satisfaction, putting down her pen. "Finally, we're getting somewhere."

"Maybe and maybe not," Jack felt compelled to point out. He didn't want Lynn giving the Montgomerys false hope. "She didn't say anything about coming home."

"But she called you and that's a start. At least we know she's alive and well—for the moment, anyway." She paused. "And then, too, maybe you're not the only person she called last night. I'm going to keep checking out her friends, someone might know something."

Jack hoped so. "You'll let me know if you find out anything?" he asked.

Her brows lifted archly. "What if I get my information in a manner that doesn't meet your standards?"

It was all Jack could do to suppress a wince. *Touché,* he thought.

"Besides, I thought you wanted to stay out of it," she reminded him, unable to completely withhold an impudent smile.

"I did," he countered just as coolly, returning her confident look. "But that was before she called me. Now I think it might be a good idea for me to see her."

Lynn nodded, mulling over his change of mind. Her face softened. "You do care about her, don't you?"

"I care about all my patients."

She studied him a long moment. Then, realizing she was staring, she abruptly looked away.

"How's the investigation going on the Golden Glow resort?" Jack asked.

"Very slowly," Lynn responded. "I asked a broker contact if he'd heard anything about it; he said no but would check around. He got back to me this morning to say that as far as he can tell, no one else has heard of it. It's being kept very quiet."

"I guess that's to be expected. Otherwise the price of the property they want to buy would rise dramatically."

"Exactly. I've also gotten people's names from your uncle, but that was just yesterday so I haven't even begun checking those out."

"Will you call me as soon as you learn anything with either case?"

Lynn gave a small sigh. She had hoped her last encounter with Jack, though it was definitely a sour one, had been the end of their involvement. She had actually looked forward to settling back down into her normal, safe, boring existence again. But here he was, insisting on being a part of her life again. Finally, she nodded. "If you promise to call me if you hear from Jessica again?"

Jack nodded. "Right away."

LYNN SAT BEHIND HER DESK, routinely logging the day's activities into the computer. Hours had passed since she'd seen Jack, yet he was still very much on her mind. She was typing some notes on Jessica, and she was justifying to herself why she had accepted Jack's offer of help. She had interviewed ten more of the young woman's friends this afternoon, but none of them had heard from her. So Jack was her only lead at the moment. She hoped that would change soon, but in the meantime, why not keep him informed? Jessica would most likely turn to him for help if she were in some kind of trouble. Why not take advantage of that?

She finished typing and pushed several more buttons. Paper fed into the printer, and within minutes her reports were printed and ready to file.

"You're really getting the hang of that computer, aren't you?" Noland said. Lynn turned around and saw him lounging in the open doorway, arms crossed over his chest.

"Slowly but surely." She sighed, not nearly as impressed as he at her skill in handling the complex machine. If only she were as adept at handling Jack, she thought. So far, they had either circled one another warily or hurled insults at each other like tempestuous teenagers. Yet she also felt an undeniable excitement every time she thought about him, a feeling that seemed to go far beyond their professional involvement. Like it or not, they probably wouldn't be finished with each other for some time.

"That Dr. Taggart who was looking for you one evening called this morning."

"He found me." Finished for the night, she walked over to her filing cabinet to put away her paperwork. She turned the lock with a decisive click.

"And?"

Briefly, Lynn explained about Jessica.

"You actually grilled his secretary?" Noland was aghast.

"Yeah, I know. But desperate people take desperate measures."

"That philosophy of yours is going to get you in trouble someday," Noland said darkly.

"It'll also help me find countless missing persons." And given that outcome, she wasn't likely to change her behavior one iota.

"I'M SORRY I DON'T HAVE better news to relate to you," Lynn told Mary and Alan Montgomery late the following morning.

The couple's spirits had been lifted by the revelation of Jessica's phone call to Jack and the knowledge she was alive, but now they were flagging again, feeling very discouraged and disillusioned.

"I told you this was a bad idea," Alan exclaimed heatedly to his wife. "We're just wasting our time and money. Jessica will come home when she wants to, if she wants to, and not a moment before."

"Money isn't the issue here," Mary responded, tears in her eyes. "Finding Jessica is, and I want my baby home."

My baby, Lynn thought. Is that really how they saw their twenty-one-year-old daughter? Or was that just the grief talking? And what kind of adult was Jessica to go off and leave her parents hurting this way? Would she come home even if she were found? Were they expecting miracles where none were possible?

Alan was unhappily silent. "I'm going back to the office," he said finally, nodding briefly to Lynn before departing. The front door closed behind him with a resounding thud.

Lynn stared after him, wondering if she was about to be fired and wondering as well if he really wanted to find his child or was just going through the motions for his wife's sake. She sensed that he had already given up on Jessica and their ability to help their daughter. That was very sad, and yet somehow fitting because whether they liked it or not, Jessica was growing up.

"So," Mary said, wiping her tears away and pulling herself together with effort, "I've been thinking about what you said about Jessie's having to find a job if she wanted to continue living independently.'' Her hands touched the single strand of pearls at her neck. ''I thought she might work in a boutique. She always did like clothes. She had a real knack for knowing exactly what to wear and how to coordinate her clothing and accessories. She used to help her friends with their wardrobes, too.''

Lynn smiled. ''Is there any place in particular that she's always liked?''

''Well, Chicago. We used to go there often when she was younger, on shopping expeditions and so forth. Do you think she could be there?'' Mary asked excitedly.

''It's possible,'' Lynn said, for the first time feeling she was beginning to make real progress on the case. ''At any rate I'll check it out.'' In the meantime, maybe they'd get some news from the phone company.

''THE CALL WAS MADE from the Atlanta airport,'' Lynn told Jack, later that day. After a visit from a police friend, the phone company had gotten that information out of their computers, and knowing Jack wanted to know the results she dropped by his office on the way home. His secretary was on the way out the door, which was good because Lynn didn't know quite what to say to her. Although in Andrea Howard's favor, she didn't seem to hold a grudge.

''Which means what?'' Jack asked, sinking down into the padded leather chair behind his desk and gesturing for her to have a seat in one of the armchairs opposite him. "Any idea where she went from there?"

"No." Lynn crossed her legs. "I've already contacted the Montgomerys and with their permission have subcontracted a detective firm in Atlanta to circulate her photo at the airport. The photos are going express mail tonight, so they'll start working on it tomorrow morning."

"Do you think they'll have any luck?"

"I don't know." She didn't believe in whitewashing the prospects just to make someone feel better momentarily. "It's hard to tell," she continued candidly, meeting his gaze. "Atlanta is a very busy airport. Thousands of people pass through there every day. If she's trying to stay lost, she could manage it there."

"Unless she uses her credit card to pay for a ticket."

"From her actions thus far, I'd say that's highly unlikely."

He scanned her summarily, his eyes a cool blue. "You don't seem depressed."

"That's because I got another lead. I'm just not sure how seriously I should take it."

He tipped back further in his chair, the motion directing her attention to the broad shoulders that were covered by a sparkling white shirt and the loosened red silk tie at his neck. His chest looked hard as a rock beneath the starched cotton. "What do you mean?"

"When I got home today from the Montgomerys there was an anonymous message on my answering machine that said Jessica had been seen at a nightclub near the university—Daisy Mae's. It's got an *Animal House* reputation and is very popular with the college crowd.''

Jack picked up a pen and turned it end over end. "You think it was on the level?"

"I don't know. It could be a prank set up by one of the college kids I've talked to the last few days. But I'm going to go there and check it out anyway." Realizing she'd kept him long enough, she clutched her purse and prepared to leave. "I just wanted to let you know about the call."

"Thanks for stopping by." He was motionless as she headed for the door. "Would you mind if I went with you to Daisy Mae's?" he asked impetuously, his low voice stopping her as she reached the portal. "I might be able to help."

Lynn hadn't been looking forward to going into that college-age, meat-counter environment alone. Of course, she was well able to defend herself after her years on the police force, so she had no fears on a physical level, but she hated being hit on. It was inevitable someone would think she was there to improve her love life. But she was determined to spend as little time as possible in Jack's company.

Lynn noticed Jack was still watching her, immersed in the telltale play of emotions on her face. Suddenly, it was all she could do not to blush or lose her composure. "Thanks for the offer," she said with equal candor, "but, uh—"

"You don't want me there," he guessed unhappily. His sensual mouth clamped into a thin line.

Lynn kept a firm rein on her impatience to be out of there. "You'd just be in the way." And she didn't need any more distractions.

"Thanks a lot," he said dryly.

She sighed her exasperation. "I'm not trying to hurt your feelings. It's just that it's wild and crazy there," she argued persuasively. "With a very young crowd."

He gave her a ruggedly appealing smile. "You don't think I'd fit in? You don't think I'd survive?"

Of course he would, but that wasn't why she didn't want him there. "In a word, no," she lied, knowing full well that if someone as undeniably handsome as Jack walked in the door, he'd be surrounded in no time by pretty young things, all looking for the thrill of experience with a gorgeous older man. But hiding her thoughts, she remarked drolly, "You're a little too yuppie. I'll call you tomorrow if anything comes up."

He stood and gave her a roguish smile that said she hadn't had the last word. "You do that."

Chapter Five

She should have known he'd show up. Lynn caught sight of Jack the moment he walked into Daisy Mae's. Ducking to avoid a glittering display of silver and gold streamers hanging on either side of the door, he made his way to the bar. Lynn angled in beside him, then waited until he'd given his order to the buxom waitress in the tattered short-shorts and low-cut red and white polka dot midriff blouse. "What are you doing here?" she hissed through a fixed smile.

His answering grin was totally unrepentant. "It's a free country. I can party anywhere I want."

He looked gorgeous. She thought he was handsome in a suit and tie, but that was nothing to the way he looked in the soft navy-blue cotton crew-necked sweater and the thigh-hugging jeans. It was obvious he had shaved and showered before coming—his dark hair was springy and soft, his skin smelled of brisk after-shave.

She felt her reaction to him all the way to her knees. When the bar stool next to her became vacant, Lynn slid onto it. She, too, ordered a drink—a Virgin Mary.

"You're interfering with my investigation."

Jack took a slow drink of the beer that was put in front of him. "Your investigation or your attempt to pick up men?" His eyes scanned her outfit. Knowing she couldn't pass for a college student if she tried, Lynn had decided on an older, more sophisticated look. Hence, she wore a glittery black sweater shot through with gold threads, a short black skirt, dark stockings and heels. The outfit was sexy and showed off her long slender legs to perfection. "I thought detectives were supposed to wear rumpled raincoats, not look as if they were on the prowl for a boyfriend."

"Not that it's any of your business—" Lynn began archly.

"The hell it isn't," he retorted evenly. "That's my patient you're trying to find."

"Ex-patient!" Lynn corrected icily, deciding then and there that she needed to be more firm in keeping Jack more than an arm's length away. "And you didn't hire me, the Montgomerys did!"

"Yeah, well, I wonder how long they'd keep you on their payroll if they learned you were putting this on their timecard," he finished grouchily. Before she could reply, he glanced over his shoulder and frowned. "People are beginning to stare. Let's dance." His hand beneath her elbow, he pulled her off the bar stool.

His action caught her by surprise. Temporarily losing her balance, she stumbled slightly, falling into his chest. The sudden closeness, the feel of his body next to hers, made her panic. But too late, his hands were already on her waist, and he was holding her so near that their lower torsos were almost touching. He swayed to the sound of the music and guided them toward the dance floor.

She wedged her arms between their chests, resisting his attempt to make her follow his steps. "Jack, I don't want to dance."

"You told me that once before," he said dryly. "But this time, I won't be refused. Besides, it's the easiest way for us to whisper together without arousing suspicion and blowing your cover." He pulled her closer, refusing to let her go, to let her even have room to breathe. Now their thighs, hips, everything were touching. And she was getting warm, impossibly warm. But short of making a tremendous scene there was nothing at all she could do.

He leaned back unexpectedly, glancing curiously down into her face. "You are under cover, aren't you?"

"I haven't exactly told everyone here I'm a private investigator, if that's what you mean," she said. "Labels like that tend to alienate potential sources, especially when they're kids and automatically resist authority at every turn."

"Then what did you tell them?"

"That I want to talk to her and I'm trying to track her down."

They were slow dancing the same way as everyone else, not stiff and formally, but in a way that closely resembled a courting clinch. It wasn't the first time she'd been held that way—far from it—but it was the first time she'd found herself in Jack's arms. They were circling the dance floor, and the soft lights, the romantic music and charged atmosphere all combined to relax her guard. She had meant to keep herself aloof, but the impact was too powerful to resist.

"I thought I asked you to stay home tonight."

He leaned back just far enough so she could see the glimmering depths of his eyes and his cocky grin. "You did. And I didn't." He tightened his arm around her waist, drawing her nearer still. His smile broadened just a little more. "So, what have you learned?"

"Nothing much. But everyone here seems to know Jessica."

"And?" His fingers splayed over her waist. She felt his restlessness and was all too aware of the sinewy movements of his thighs as they bumped hers from time to time.

Swallowing hard, she forced herself to concentrate on the subject of Jessica and not on the way his body felt pressed against the length of hers. "No one's heard from her." She wet her lips, which were unaccountably dry, as dry as her throat.

His eyes tracked the involuntary movement. "You're sure?"

Was he doubting her ability? "It's early yet. I haven't worked the entire club."

A moment passed as he considered his options, then decided on a pleasant tack. "Let me help."

This was the last thing she wanted—to have him for a partner. Catching him by surprise, she easily extricated herself from his grip and took a step back. "You can inquire all you want, on your own. But as for me, I work alone.''

Not waiting for him to reply, she walked to the end of the bar and promptly struck up a conversation with the burliest guy there, who she guessed must be a football player for the university. His shoulders, neck and chest were humongous. He made her feel like a dwarf.

In response to her question, he said, ''No, I don't know Hilary Martin.'' His eyes lingered on Lynn's clinging jersey sweater, with its modest neck and long sleeves. ''Want to dance?''

If that was the only way to keep him talking. ''Sure.'' She got up, gliding easily into his arms. He held her as Jack had, but this felt more like a violation of her space than an act of socialization. Nonetheless, she needed answers. Gritting her teeth, she plastered on a smile and asked brightly, ''What about Tamara Powell?''

''No, her neither.'' He squinted. ''You sure you're not a teacher?''

Now she did feel old. ''Just an ex-student. From another college.''

''Oh. Well.'' He smiled. ''You're pretty, you know that?''

''Thank you.'' As he whirled her around, she caught a glimpse of Jack's face. Though surrounded by college-age girls, all of whom seemed hopelessly impressed, he gave her a grim look. She ignored it and turning back to the jock, she asked nonchalantly, ''What about Jessica Montgomery?''

His eyes lit up. "Yeah, I know her. But she quit—"

"I know. before the fall term ever started. But I wanted to look her up anyway."

"Oh." He was silent, thinking.

"Do you know where I can find her?"

The massive shoulders lifted and fell. "Not exactly."

"What does that mean?"

He squinted down at her affably. "Well, the guys and me—we're on the team—we had this bet going last night. There was some girl in here and she looked like Jessica, you know, but she didn't look like her."

"What do you mean?"

"She was just real quiet, you know. And Jess was always the life of the party. This girl, she was just kind of sitting there at one of the tables in the back, observing."

"Did she seem—" Lynn almost said depressed, then caught herself and said, "Out of it?"

"Drunk? Hell, no. This girl wasn't drinking anything except 7-Up."

"Did you talk to her? I mean maybe they were cousins or something?" To have Jessica in town at the precise moment Lynn was looking for her seemed almost too good to be true, especially when she'd already been gone six weeks. Maybe there was something to that anonymous message that had been left on her answering machine.

"I was going to, but by the time I got over there she had already taken off." His arms tightened around her waist. He pulled her closer. "But let's not talk about

Jessica. Let's talk about you and me, babe, and where we're going to go after this." He tightened his hold on her, hugging her closer, until she thought her ribs would crack.

Lynn was about to excuse herself to go the ladies' room when a hand tapped the jock on the back.

"Excuse me," Jack said, smiling. "I'm cutting in."

The bruiser looked perturbed. "You want to dance with him?"

No, Lynn thought, but she would, anything to get away from the burly guy she was with. "He's an old acquaintance," Lynn said. "I really think I should."

The bruiser let her go after a long consideration.

"You can sigh your relief now." Jack said as soon as he was gone.

Lynn was irritated he had so easily read her mind. Her spine stiffened. "What makes you think I'd want to do that?"

Jack grinned, looking victorious. She told herself she couldn't fathom why. "That pasty color on your face when your athlete there began to make his move," he said smoothly, whirling her around. The music had turned fast, but he showed no signs of releasing his grip on her waist. He merely had changed his steps, altering them to fit the quick beat.

Lynn felt new color flood her cheeks. "He wasn't—"

"Bull!" He stared at her with utter disbelief. "You were out of your league and you know it."

"Thanks for the memories." She wedged her arms between their chests.

"Oh, don't play so hard to get." He showed no signs of letting her go.

She stiffened, refusing to let him take advantage of her, or the situation. "I think you should let me go now." Or she would make a scene. Already heads were turning in their direction.

Jack shook his head and merely tightened his grip. He bent his head low until his voice whispered enticingly into her ear. "Not until you tell me what Bozo the Bruiser there said."

Lynn sighed. As curious and insistent as Jack was proving to be, he'd no doubt find out anyway. Besides maybe this was something he should know in case Jessica called again. She repeated her conversation with the jock, murmuring conscientiously, and reassured herself that the unmistakably flirtatious looks she was being forced to give him now were all for show, for the people she knew were watching them still.

"Do you think it was her?" Jack asked.

Lynn shrugged, watching the action on the dance floor. The later it got, the more people were pairing up. "I don't know. Maybe she does really want to come back. After six weeks, she's probably almost out of money. But then maybe she's afraid to go home."

"Because of the way she left?"

"She might figure her parents are angry with her."

"You want to tell the Montgomerys what you've found out?"

Lynn was glad to see he was caring about the feelings of the family, who often went through more emotional trauma just waiting and wondering and worrying, than the runaways themselves. "I don't know. It seems a bit premature when all we have is a rumor to go on. I think we'd better wait to get some kind of confirmation before we say anything to the Montgomerys. I don't want to get their hopes up if it's not true. That would be too cruel."

He nodded, thinking. "I agree," he said finally, looking first serious, then rather pleased.

"You don't have to look so surprised," she commented before she could stop herself. "I do have some judgment."

"I guess so. Although," Jack continued in a light tone, "I never would have figured it when you were dancing with Bozo the Bruiser."

He knew he sounded as if he was teasing her, but the truth was it was very hard for him to see her in another man's arms. What was more, as much as she might want to deny it, he knew she was falling prey to the same deluge of feelings that were overwhelming him. He didn't fully understand all the reasons why he was so attracted to her; he didn't need to. He was old enough to understand that what happened between a man and a woman wasn't always logical, and it never happened when it was expected. For now it was enough for him that the chemistry between them was there.

But he couldn't keep his thoughts from straying to the future, to the possibilities that existed between them. An affair with Lynn would be passionate, he was sure, and definitely hard won. She'd resist every step of the way, like she was doing now, and when she wasn't doing that, she would very likely be doing something that would infuriate him. But he was determined to have her someday.

The song ended, and this time, he released her. Lynn went back to her questioning of the club's patrons—to no avail. No one else there had spotted Jessica, if indeed it had been Jessica there the previous night.

From the looks of it, Jack didn't seem to be having any better luck. Aware it was almost closing time, Lynn was about to go home when she was approached by Chad Bryson. He was president of the university's most prestigious fraternity, and she knew from just looking at him that he was probably as spoiled, reckless and rich as Jessica. He had blond hair cut in an unusual style with bangs that dipped low over one eye. He had also been purposefully eluding her all night, to her frustration, which made her wonder what had changed his mind about talking to her.

"I heard you've been asking about Jessica Montgomery," Chad began easily, taking a seat next to her at the bar.

Lynn knew Chad had dated Jessica several years ago. His picture had been given to her by Mary Montgomery. "I'd like to talk to her." Lynn studied him, not sure whether she could trust him. On the surface, of course, everything was faultless. He was wearing a navy Cerruti blazer, a white shirt and silk tie, stonewashed designer jeans. A gold Rolex was on his wrist. He also had a cocky self-assurance she disliked and bedroom eyes and a suave manner that bordered on sleaze. But he knew something; she could tell that just by looking at him. If it weren't for that, she wouldn't even have spoken to him.

Abruptly, he said, "You want to know about Jessica? Meet me by the back door in two minutes." Then he spun on his heel and walked away.

Lynn stared after him, already knowing what she was going to do. She hadn't ever gotten anywhere without taking a risk or two. She wouldn't stop now.

IT WAS NEAR CLOSING TIME when Jack saw Lynn slip out the back door of Daisy Mae's. Curious, and ticked off that she hadn't even said goodbye to him, he slipped out the side entrance and caught a glimpse of her getting into the low-slung white Maserati without a backward glance. She was with that fraternity boy he'd seen her chasing unsuccessfully all night, the boy who looked as if he were made of money and would never do an honest day's work. And now it was 2:00 a.m., and Lynn was going off somewhere with him in his fancy car.

Let her go, Jack thought, sternly schooling himself to remain emotionally uninvolved. *It's none of my business what she'll do to get information, or how far she'll go.* But if that kid by some chance did lead her to Jessica... As depressed and anxious as she'd sounded the other night on the phone, she might need his help.

His decision made, Jack sprinted through the near-empty parking lot to his car and climbed in. Two blocks later, he caught sight of the white Maserati gleaming in the distance. Pressing his foot harder on the gas pedal, he began to speed up.

"YOU SAID YOU WERE GOING to take me to Jessica," Lynn said sternly when Chad guided his car into the parking lot and braked beneath a neon sign of hot pink and sizzling blue. She didn't like being jerked around, and at two in the morning, it was an unspeakable thing to do to someone.

"And I mean to keep that promise," Chad said with an ease that irritated her.

Lynn shot a glance at the sign up above. "By taking me to the Restful Nite motel?"

"What? You don't like the location?" He pretended surprise.

I don't like you, Lynn thought. "Look, if this is a game," she said with weary anger, starting to get out of the car, "it's over." She'd go into the motel office and call a cab.

He caught her wrist before she could open the door. "It's no game," he said seriously. "I talked to Jessica last night."

Something in his face made her believe him. "Why didn't you tell me this earlier?"

"Because I didn't trust you. I'm not sure I do now, either. Are you a cop?" He narrowed his eyes.

"No," Lynn said carefully.

Chad released her slowly. "Is Jessie in trouble?"

Lynn could see that despite the bad-boy image he worked hard to exude, Chad genuinely cared about

Jessica. "Only in that she's alone and her parents are very worried about her."

Recognition dawned. The bedroom eyes turned calculating and not particularly receptive. "You're a private investigator, then?" he said, not bothering to hide his loathing of her profession.

"Yes. What did Jessica say when you saw her?"

He shrugged. "That she was homesick."

"Anything else?"

He was silent.

"Was she staying here in the city? Planning to see her folks? Is she living here somewhere now or even looking for a place?"

"Cool it with all the questions, will you? I don't know the answers anyway. She didn't really seem to want to talk last night and I don't blame her. Dropping out of school and all. It's a major embarrassment for her as well as her folks."

With friends like Chad, who needs enemies? Lynn thought. But at least he cared enough about Jessica to talk to Lynn.

"I need to talk to her." Lynn looked over at the motel, which at best seemed a breeding ground for lice. "Is she staying here?" Somehow she couldn't imagine the pampered blond heiress doing so.

"What do you think?" he asked dryly.

"That you've led me on a wild-goose chase." She spoke with a calm, authoritative tone of voice, knowing she had to show him that she was in control of the situation.

"You're very smart." He smiled at her, his glance turning slightly licentious.

Ignoring his come-hither glance, Lynn looked around, wishing she had her car and that they hadn't ended up in such a sleazy part of town. No doubt, as sure of himself as he was, he'd thought to seduce her as well as lead her on a merry almost fruitless chase. But, she thought triumphantly, she had a second validation that Jessica had been in Indianapolis for at least one night. And that was a very positive sign.

"So?" Chad grinned lazily, leaning back against the car door. "What do you say? Want to get a room?"

In your dreams, pal. Lynn fought the urge to laugh, his request was so outlandish. If he thought he was going to take advantage of her, he had another think coming. Reaching into her purse, she pulled out an aerosol can of mace. "My brother's a cop. So's my dad," she said sweetly, pretending to inspect the directions on the back of the can. "And at one time, I was, too." She looked at him, this time not bothering to hide her icy determination to end the interview promptly. "So, if you've told me all you can, I'd like to be taken back to my car. Right now."

He eyed the can of mace, weighed what she said, then sighed dramatically. He thrust the car into gear. "Anything you say," he said dejectedly.

"CHANGE IN PLANS?"

Lynn turned to see Jack emerge from his car. They were standing alone in the Daisy Mae's parking lot.

"You followed us." But he hadn't appeared until after Chad had driven off, wheels screeching.

"You noticed."

"Right." Although to be truthful, she hadn't until they were almost back at the club.

"That kid tell you anything helpful?"

"Yes and no." Lynn explained.

"So now what?" Jack sighed, frustrated by the slow unfolding of the investigation. "Do we call it a night?"

She picked up on his *we*, refusing to admit to herself how it warmed her soul. "I don't know," she said honestly, trying to decide. She ought to be home in bed. But after the night she'd had, she knew sleep was a long way off. And besides, she had one more errand to do. She looked at Jack speculatively. "Feel like a run back to the Restful Nite motel?"

He was apparently up for anything and also recognized the chance to get his answers. "Why not?" he said dryly. "Since I've been begging to be included in this all night. Your car or mine?"

"Mine."

As she drove through the deserted downtown streets, Lynn asked, "Why'd you follow us?" She had been surprised to see his car behind the Maserati, and felt indignant because that meant he thought she needed watching over. How could he not think she was fully capable of taking care of herself. Then she wondered why he didn't actually meddle when they were in the motel parking lot.

"I thought you might need help."

"But you didn't interfere."

"You seemed to be handling him just fine."

"Thanks."

"Although I still don't understand why he drove you all the way to the Restful Nite motel just to tell you what he did."

"I know, that's been bugging me, too. But then I got to thinking," Lynn said as she pulled into the motel parking lot and turned the motor off. She faced Jack with a quizzical expression on her face. "Maybe he initially meant to do a little more than just talk to me tonight."

"Like what? Check in with you?" The words spilled out before Jack could stop himself.

She grinned at his shocked and penitent look. "Nicely put, but no, I don't think so. Instead, perhaps it's because Jessica really is here," Lynn mused, climbing out of the car and leaving Jack to follow.

Minutes later, Lynn had her validation. The desk clerk readily identified Jessica from a picture. "Sure she was here," he said. "Checked in sometime yesterday afternoon, and out again late last night."

"When?"

"About ten-thirty or so. Said she had a plane to catch."

"Did she say where?" Lynn tried to contain her excitement.

"No. Just that she wanted to get out of town. Seemed in a hurry, too."

Jack swore beneath his breath. Knowing the clerk had told them all he could, Lynn thanked him and gave him her number in case he thought of anything else.

She and Jack walked back out to her car. "Are you hungry by any chance?" she asked.

"As a matter of fact, yeah."

"I know an all-night coffee shop not far from here. Want to go with me? We could compare notes on what happened earlier." And a well-lit restaurant seemed more conducive to a business discussion than her dimly lit car.

"Sure. Why not?"

They drove in silence and minutes later, when they were seated and had placed their orders, Lynn asked, "So what did you find out?"

"Not much," Jack admitted openly, not pleased with his lack of progress. "One girl I talked to said she might have seen Jessica last night, but that if it was her, she'd changed her hair. Cut it and lightened it a little. She also had a pretty good tan."

"Hm." She hadn't expected him to do any better actually. "I wonder why she would have stayed at the Restful Nite motel? Could it be because she didn't want to be seen? No one would connect Jessica the heiress with the Restful Nite motel."

"True," Jack sighed. "I have a hard time envisioning her there myself." He looked concerned again, troubled and discouraged.

"You really care about her, don't you?"

"I'm protective of all my patients." He leaned back, silent, as the waitress put their plates in front of them. Ham and eggs and hash browns for her, pie and coffee for Jack. "So what next?" he asked earnestly the moment the waitress was gone.

"I'm going to go to the airport first thing tomorrow morning, see if I can find out if Jessica did leave town again, and if so, where she went. After that, I have an appointment with her former roommate."

"You haven't talked to her yet?"

"She's student teaching this semester. It's the first time she could fit me in, though she's already said she doesn't know what she could say. But we'll see. And then after that, I have an appointment with her school advisor."

"You're not leaving any stone unturned."

"Not if I can help it."

Again, he was quiet. "I really would like to help."

Lynn looked at him. She wanted to keep plenty of distance between them, but he seemed determined to keep closing in. "I suppose if I tell you no you'll just show up there tomorrow anyway?" she said dryly.

"I feel a responsibility since she was my patient. It's not normal operating procedure for me, but then again I don't want anything to happen to Jessica."

"So to salve your conscience you'll continue." She meant to say it sarcastically, but somehow it came out a compliment.

He nodded slowly, looking suddenly as if he still had some mixed feelings about getting involved at all. Again he put them aside, injecting a determined cheerfulness into his tone. "Tomorrow then? I have only one appointment and can reschedule it."

Lynn nodded, her expression suddenly serious. This was business, mutual concern over a runaway. And that was all it was, despite the dancing, despite the protective vibes she'd sensed coming from him earlier. "I'll get started about nine. If you want to go with me," she finished briskly, "don't be late."

Chapter Six

He not only was on time, he was fifteen minutes early. They headed immediately for the airport, and by splitting up, they covered twice the territory in half the time. Though several ticket agents thought the picture of Jessica looked vaguely familiar, no one could say for sure that she had bought a ticket or even been at the airport Thursday evening. Nor was her name on any passenger list of any flights out.

Fortunately the interview with her former roommate went slightly better. A gregarious young woman with flame-red hair, Wendy Archer hadn't heard from Jessica, but she had plenty to say about Jessica's state of mind before she ran away.

"Jessica was really unhappy. She felt her parents had her life all mapped out for her, that nobody cared about what she wanted. They just had all these expectations. The guys all wanted to date her because she was an heiress. I guess running away was the only way she could escape from all that," she concluded.

"Then you don't think she's run away just to live in the fast lane?" With kids from wealthy families, Lynn knew that was always a possibility.

"I don't think so. She could have done that here and gone to all the A-list parties. Besides, the social life at the sorority is great, so why move on? No, if she left, it was because she wanted to get away. From everything."

"Well, on to the next interview," Lynn said when they left the sorority house.

"Maybe her advisor will know more," Jack said hopefully.

A harried-looking gentlemen in his late forties, Mr. Smead was gracious and gregarious. "Sure I remember Jessica. Pretty girl, though I'm not sure she really belonged in the school of business. To tell you the truth, she didn't seem all that interested in the field."

"Did Jessica ever talk to you about changing her major?" Lynn said, settling back in her seat.

"No. The only thing we ever talked about at length was her fear of public speaking. She ended up in a drama class or two, and it seemed to do the trick for her."

"Was she happy then?"

Mr. Smead sighed. "I think—and this is strictly off the record—that she was being pushed into the wrong field. I understand why her parents wanted her to get an education in business, but the fact of the matter was Jessica was no businessperson. And I think she knew it and hated feeling inadequate. She needed to find herself."

Maybe she'd done just that, Lynn thought. It was clear that this was part of the reason why she'd run away and maybe also why she wasn't coming back. Not yet, but soon, Lynn hoped.

"So now what?" Jack asked after they'd left the professor.

"Next, we go to the Montgomerys'." Lynn jangled her car keys, trying not to notice how easily she and Jack walked together, their strides almost perfectly matched. They were getting along well, but only because they had a common goal and a newfound sense of cooperation. It had nothing to do with them personally, and it certainly wasn't indicative of any chemistry existing between them Lynn told herself firmly.

"So you think she left town again?" Mary asked tearfully.

"Looks that way," Lynn admitted sadly. She wished she had better news to give.

Alan looked at Jack. "What do you make of all this, Dr. Taggart?"

Jack was quiet. Lynn could tell he hated being put on the spot, but he had to accept the fact that he was involved now. "She may be trying to work up the nerve to come home. I'd say her visit here to Indianapolis means she's considering it." All in all, he felt that was a good sign.

"She mentioned to Chad she was homesick," Lynn added, reinforcing what Jack had said.

Mary took comfort in that. "I miss her, too. We both do. You'll keep on searching for her?" she asked.

"Oh, yes," Lynn promised. "We, I mean I, won't stop until I find her."

Satisfied progress was being made, the Montgomerys bid them goodbye.

"It's ironic," Jack commented as they were walking to the car, "but I kind of like being included in your work."

Lynn blushed. She'd known he would bring up that "we." She couldn't imagine how she'd made such a Freudian slip, and to a psychiatrist, no less. "Considering the way we started out, it is ironic," she agreed, keeping her tone light and her eyes averted. "Maybe you just have investigative work in your blood."

"So what are your plans for the rest of the day?" he asked as they reached the car. There was a husky catch to his voice.

"What do you mean?" she asked.

He gave her a look. "It is Saturday. Do you normally work all weekend long?"

A glance at her watch indicated it was only three o'clock. They still had the rest of the afternoon ahead of them. "When I have a job and a lead to follow up, yes," she answered his question dutifully. Then she sighed wearily, thinking back to the hectic hours they had spent today and last night. "Right now I have a tired brain, and I still have to do some following up on your uncle's case."

His gaze took in the slight disarray of her golden hair, falling around her shoulders. "Maybe you just need a break for inspiration to strike again and energy to come back," he said gently. He was quiet a moment, thinking. Then he turned on his smile and his charm in a way that was strictly man to woman. "I had planned to drive out to Mansfield Lake this afternoon. I've got a houseboat docked out there. Want to come?"

She couldn't deny she was really tempted. It was a perfect Indian summer day. If she went home now, she'd stay indoors all day, glued to her computer and phone. Not a very exciting way to spend the weekend.

"You want to go. I can tell by the look in your eyes," he teased.

How easily he saw into her! Now, if she said she didn't want to, he'd know she'd be lying.

"Say yes." He took a step toward her.

Her senses flooded at his nearness. "Jack—" The word ended in a soft, strangled moan in her throat as he took her hand and gently pulled her closer.

"It's not a date. If you don't want it to be one, then it won't be." He smiled roguishly. "I promise I won't even try to kiss you."

"You're not making it easy for me to do my work for your uncle." She felt the heat of a blush warm her cheeks, and knew she was fighting a losing battle, trying to stay emotionally aloof from this man. Like it or not, he got to her every time. And whenever he touched her...

"I don't intend to make your refusal of my invitation easy on you, either. Come on, you need some time off."

What could it hurt? she asked herself. Especially when he was right about her needing a break. Besides, he'd done his best to help her find Jessica. Why shouldn't she do something for him that he so obviously wanted her to do?

"All right." She heard herself accepting his invitation before she could talk herself out of it. This once she would follow her impulse, just go with the flow. "I'd like that very much."

He smiled again, this time looking very pleased with himself.

THEY PICKED UP HIS CAR and his keys to the houseboat. Jack drove as effortlessly as he did everything else, and she relaxed beside him, letting someone else take charge for a little while. "So do you do this often?" she asked.

"Take the boat out? Sure, whenever I can." He frowned slightly, before slanting her a friendly glance. "But I didn't always." Again, he was silent, then added, "After my divorce I lost myself in my work, too."

She looked out at the passing scenery, wishing life were easier, hers and his. "What happened to make you change your hardworking ways?" In an effort to inject lightness into the conversation she made her tone droll.

Jack sighed and gave her a lopsided smile before turning his attention once again to the road. "I ended up alone on Christmas Eve. I'd promised my parents I would fly out to Arizona, which is where they live, but then I got sidetracked at work and forgot to make airline reservations. I didn't remember until it was too late to get a flight out. I even went to the airport and tried to go standby but that didn't work. So I spent the holiday alone. It was pretty dismal. Everyone else I knew here had already made plans. I realized then how much I'd let my personal and social life slide. Anyway, it was a helluva way to spend a holiday.''

"I guess so." She knew he was trying, in a round-about well-intentioned way, to caution her not to work so hard. She realized guiltily she hadn't taken enough time off recently. She'd been so eager to get her business going that when she wasn't actually on a case, she was out trying to drum up business by passing out flyers. And that wasn't good. Everyone, no matter how efficient and energetic they were, needed breaks.

Jack guided the car onto a narrow paved road, slowing as they approached the placid blue water. "What was your life like before the divorce?" she asked casually as he parked in the lot next to the small privately owned marina. "Were you a workaholic then, too?"

"No," Jack said, pocketing the car keys and climbing out of the car. "But my wife was. In all the time we were married, which was almost seven years, she was never able to separate her work from our personal life."

Lynn fell into step beside him, lengthening her stride slightly to keep pace. "What kind of work did she do?"

"She was a social worker." Jack waved to a neighboring boater—one of the few people out that day—and then climbed into the twenty-eight-foot boat with an enclosed cabin. Painted red and white, it had the word *Freedom* painted on the side. He leaned down and gave her a hand up onto the deck. "I didn't mind her caring about her cases, but she took it way beyond what was necessary. She used to meddle constantly in other people's lives. Consequently, she had no time for our marriage."

"You resented that?" Lynn gave him a hand untying the ropes.

"Yeah, a lot." Jack unlocked the interior of the boat and slid into the captain's seat behind the wheel. He paused, his hands on the wheel, a distressed look on his face. Then he said softly but sadly, "I didn't realize how much, though, until way later, until there was no more ignoring it, if you know what I mean."

Lynn did and she nodded sympathetically, slipping into a seat beside him.

"I just knew it wasn't working out, that our marriage wasn't what either of us expected it to be, and that hence we were both unhappy, depressed."

"So there were no regrets?" Lynn asked softly, knowing it was important to her that Jack had wanted and accepted the divorce as inevitable.

"No regrets," Jack said unemotionally. "Just relief." He sighed, and then continued, "As far as endings go, ours was pretty grim. We fought constantly. I wanted a future. She was too busy solving problems for everyone else to even think about us."

"So what happened?" Lynn found her mouth was dry.

He shrugged as if it no longer mattered. "One day I came home and found she'd packed up all her things and moved in with a friend," he related tiredly. "A guy from the agency."

"That must have hurt," Lynn said gently, her heart going out to him. At least in the breakup of her own marriage, there'd been no third party, no adulterous slap in the face.

"Not as much as I would have expected. Mostly, I was glad it was finally over, that I didn't have to try to work out the impossible anymore. Know what I mean?"

"I think so," Lynn said slowly. Though her own divorce had come about much more dramatically, she, too, had felt a sense of relief when it was all over, a sense of freedom that had been at times almost giddy, and yet at the same time very sad. She studied him pensively and wondered if he had any lingering feelings for his ex-wife.

"I think the divorce was for the best, but I'm sorry my marriage failed," he admitted honestly, his eyes serious in the dim light of the cabin. "My parents have a good marriage and I wanted the same for myself."

"Then you are planning to get married again someday?" Lynn asked before she could think.

"Yeah, sure." He gave her a slow sexy grin. "Providing of course I find the right woman." Briefly, his gaze roved over her face, lingering on her mouth before returning to her eyes. "What about you?"

"I don't know," she said honestly. Although for the very first time she was beginning to consider dating seriously again. "I'd have to see." Certainly, she wanted to be with someone who understood her commitment to her work, her unusual hours. Someone flexible and understanding. Someone as attractive and interesting as Jack Taggart.

He turned his full attention to the boat, started the motor and guided it out of the slip. As it glided slowly farther out into the lake, Lynn looked around, noting that Jack couldn't have picked a more restful place as a weekend getaway. The trees surrounding the glistening blue water were beautiful, their foliage yellow, red, silver and orange. In the distance against the muted blue of the sky another boat could be seen. She guessed they were also out for a quiet Saturday afternoon.

"A penny for your thoughts," Jack teased, dropping anchor.

Lynn stood at the rail, feeling the gentle autumn breeze through her hair. "I was just thinking what a beautiful day it is."

"And no doubt how glad you are I talked you into coming." His low voice was underscored with humor. Yet he looked so vulnerable, as if it was important to him that she liked being with him. She felt a catch at her heart.

"That, too," she said softly. Suddenly, she realized how much ground they had gained in so little time. They'd started out enemies—or almost—and now were nearer to being friends. There was still a lot she didn't know about him, but there was already much she liked and was attracted to. His strength of character, for one thing. His compassion for his patients, another. He was smart, sensitive, and not easy to read. He seemed to be a man who sometimes played his cards very close to his vest and that intrigued her; she would have liked to know what was on his mind all the time. But she couldn't help wondering if she was letting herself get in a little too deep, considering that they were at odds over her sleuthing methods. She should never let herself get involved with a man who didn't fully respect what she did.

He studied her introspective expression. "Sure your mind isn't still on your work?" he asked gently.

"No. I was thinking about something else." Something troubling. She took a deep breath, knowing she should reassure him before he became suspicious, and at the same time let him understand her a little better. "If anything, in the past, I've tended to go the opposite way," she admitted honestly, "and not let the emotional ramifications of a situation get to me at all."

"What do you mean?" Suddenly he seemed wary, on edge.

She stared out at the sky, again feeling the restlessness and turmoil of her past. She looked at him, wanting him to accept her flaws as well as her strengths. "When I was a policewoman, it was very difficult for me, especially at first. I think it's natural to get emotionally involved with the people you're assigned to help. And yet to survive, you have to keep a certain distance and perspective.''

"We doctors do that, too.''

"Yes, well, the way I did that was by building walls around myself, becoming almost completely numb to people and their pain. It was either that or give in to the frustration of never being able to do quite enough, especially in missing persons cases.''

"That's the area where you were assigned?''

"Yes, at first.''

"Were you as tenacious then as you are now?'' Curiosity and something closely akin to disapproval deepened the blue of his eyes.

"Yes and no,'' Lynn said, brushing the hair from her cheeks. She felt herself blush. "At first, I was relentless. I railed against every rule and regulation. I was going to find the answer no matter what.''

"Then what happened?''

"I burned out. I got to the point where I simply accepted every rule as gospel. If they said I couldn't do it, I couldn't do it. Period. End of case.'' Lynn's mouth tightened unhappily as she remembered how callously she behaved for that short period of time. It had been a question of survival on her part. She did what she had to in order to go on, but it wasn't easy remembering how rigid she was toward the people who needed her help. In a soft voice underscored with regret, she continued, "Later, after a couple of particularly difficult cases that didn't have such happy endings, I began to realize I had become a hindrance rather than a help.'' She was silent a moment. "I realized then that I didn't want to go through the rest of my life forced to shut off my feelings and instincts. I didn't want to be quite so hampered by rules and regulations when I was trying to find a missing child or a teenage runaway.''

"And that's when you quit the force and opened your own agency?" Jack guessed.

More or less. "Yes," Lynn said.

"Has it helped, being your own boss?" He came and stood next to her.

Lynn looked at him. "Yes," she said quietly. "I still struggle sometimes. My initial tendency is always to walk away from sticky situations, to just not want to get involved." Jack looked surprised. "But once I pass that threshold of resistance," Lynn warned, "I'm always able to do my job and do it well. So now I don't have to look back with regret at the cases I handle. If I don't find someone it's not because I haven't tried every way possible."

"You do love your work, don't you?" Jack said softly, understanding how she felt, if not completely approving of everything she did.

Lynn nodded. "The satisfaction I feel at the successful conclusion of a case is more than enough to carry me through the dark moments." And there were many of those.

"I know what you mean," he said gently. "My work has plenty of ups and downs, too. But helping just one person can make up for a lot."

Yes, it could, Lynn thought. She stared up at him, amazed at how close she felt to him. "I never thought we'd have so much in common," she murmured.

"The truth? Initially, neither did I. But we do," he said slowly, his eyes roving over her face once again, this time with mesmerizing intensity. She looked up into his eyes and felt herself melting inside.

"Glad you came out here today?" he asked.

She nodded, so aware of him she could barely breathe.

"So am I."

And then she knew. Something was happening here.

Jack knew it, too. Wordlessly, giving her no chance to resist or even react, he closed the distance between them, taking her by the shoulders. His head was lowering, his lips slanting over hers. She breathed in the crisp, woodsy scent of his cologne, and her palms flattened over the muscled contours of his chest, unsure of whether she was resisting or urging him on. She only knew she wanted to touch him, and that he made her feel more like a woman than she had in months.

"I told myself when I asked you out here today I wouldn't do this. I lied," he said simply, his warm breath brushing her lips. His hands cupped her shoulders and he pulled her closer, until thigh touched thigh, until her breasts were crushed against the hardness of his chest. "I am going to kiss you."

And she was going to kiss him back. His hands slid into her hair, tilting her head up. Their lips merged and Lynn felt a jolt all the way to her toes. He kissed her as if she were the first, with heat and pressure and a tenderness that robbed her of breath and the will or the need to think. She was here in his arms, and nothing had ever felt so right. His lips muffling the soft sound of her enjoyment, she struggled to cling to the edge of reason. It was impossible. His kiss was deep and slow and more arousing than anything she'd ever known. She felt weak with surrender. She opened her mouth at his urging, returning kiss after insatiable kiss, until she was filled with an incredible wanting, the insatiable need to touch, to taste. And touch again. He became even more gentle and she arched against him, savoring the embrace, her hands smoothing over his back.

The kiss was everything, but it had to end. They both knew it. They were trembling as they drew apart.

She felt stunned and wary.

"I'm rushing you, aren't I?" Jack asked.

Lynn nodded, relieved to be able to admit the truth. "Yes." Things were moving along at an alarming pace. She wasn't prepared for the passion and the gloriously alive way he made her feel. She met his glance and felt as if she were wearing her heart on her sleeve. But she wasn't the only one vulnerable here. They both had a lot at stake. Suddenly she knew he wouldn't take advantage of her, and she began to relax.

He looked up at the sky. Storm clouds were gathering on the far horizon. "I guess we'd better get the *Freedom* back in."

"Guess so."

"Want to come out here again sometime?" he asked, pulling up the anchor. He switched on the motor, and the engine came to life.

The question was innocent enough. After a moment, Lynn nodded. Yes, she did. But she just didn't know if she should.

"So how've you been?" Lynn asked Theresa early Sunday afternoon. Theresa had called Lynn and invited her to go to the playground with her and Carter. Lynn had agreed to go because she hadn't spent time with Theresa in so long.

Now, watching Carter playing happily on the wooden fort—complete with slides and swings—she noted how happy and content both he and Theresa looked.

"Great, actually," Theresa replied, her green eyes sparkling. "I met a man," she continued, explaining the reason for her newfound euphoria. "His name is Roy Johnson. He's a teacher at the high school. Oh, Lynn, he's so nice! And we get along so well, we agree about almost everything! I can hardly believe my good fortune!"

Lynn smiled, wishing she were as lucky. She'd met a man she was very attracted to all right, but she and Jack didn't begin to agree on everything. "How did you meet him?" she asked, sitting down on a nearby park bench.

"At a volunteer training session for the Red Cross." She stretched her blue-jeaned legs out in front of her. "I signed up to be on a disaster team a couple of weeks ago. You know I do that every year, but this is the first time I met someone. Boy, am I glad I went!''

''He's that terrific?'' Lynn asked, suddenly wishing her life was going as smoothly as Theresa's.

''And then some.''

''Does Carter like him?''

Theresa studied her son affectionately, watching as he walked backward up the slide. ''Oh, yes, very much. And Roy likes Carter, too. They get along so great you'd almost think they were father and son.''

Lynn looked at her friend. Theresa did have a special glow about her. She wondered if she were falling in love with Roy, and if so, if they would eventually get married.

Lynn was happy for her but she was also disturbed. She had to protect them all from Theresa's past curiosity about the health of Carter's biological father. Her peace of mind had been restored because Jack was healthy, but in exchange for that Lynn had the burden of knowing something she never should have been asked to discover. As long as those case files existed, even though they were locked up in a drawer, Lynn admitted she was a little nervous. She didn't want anyone ever finding out what she had learned. There was only one way to make sure it never happened and that was by destroying the files. After all, she didn't need them anymore. It was a closed case, over and done with.

Lynn returned home and went into her office. She went to the file cabinet, unlocked it, and removed the paper files on Jack. Methodically, she shredded them into tiny bits of paper. She then erased the files on the two computer diskettes where the information had also been stored, and rechecked them thoroughly to ensure that they were now blank, which they were.

She carried all the paper remains to the fireplace and fed them into the fire. She stayed until the last shredded piece was charred black, then gave a final, weary sigh of relief. Finally she was at peace with herself. She had done the right thing in protecting Theresa and her son and Jack. She was sparing them all a great deal of pain. Now that the information was destroyed, it was truly over. No one would ever have to know.

Chapter Seven

"Wow, I am impressed," Jack exclaimed. He and Lynn were in the formal dining room of Sheila's home, and they were looking over layouts, drawings and photos of the proposed Golden Glow resort.

"It seems like it has just about everything," Lynn said.

Sheila came up to them and stood beside Walter. She was hosting the affair, an informal presentation for people interested in investing in the project. She'd been busy all afternoon with refreshments and carried a slightly damp tea towel in her hand. "I especially like the hike and bike trails that wind around the property. We're going to plant wildflowers all over, so it should be especially beautiful in the spring," she said energetically, unable to contain her enthusiasm.

"Yeah, it will be," Walter agreed. "We're even thinking of having a full-time sex therapist like Dr. Ruth there. You know, to help out with—"

"Uncle Walter!" Jack interrupted sternly. Walter only chuckled at Lynn's shocked expression.

Rolling her eyes up, Sheila went back into the kitchen. Lynn tagged along to see if she could help and to find out more about the business expertise and instincts that Sheila had unexpectedly been demonstrating all afternoon with her answers to some of the questions raised by others.

Jack was left standing with his uncle, and he picked up the aerial photos of the property that the Golden Glow backers had their eyes on. Part was farmland that had been put up for auction; other parts were either heavily treed or overgrown pastureland.

Walter frowned, regarding his nephew. "You're still a doubting Thomas?"

"I'm sorry, but yes, I am. I just want this to go right," he answered quietly.

"So do I," Walter responded.

"I WAS SURPRISED that most of their backers don't have much of a business background," Lynn said an hour later as she and Jack entered his condo. During the drive there, she had been updating him on her Golden Glow investigation. "They're retired teachers and nurses and mostly women, just like all those women who were at Sheila's this afternoon. Widows with some money put away. And that bothers me."

"I know what you mean," Jack replied. "It would be easier to feel confident if they had at least one experienced builder or developer for an investor." They walked into the living room and sat down on the sofa. Jack took off his shoes and propped his feet on the coffee table. "I do think the idea is great. Older people need places to go where they can have fun and meet other older people.''

"With your uncle there the atmosphere's bound to be a little reminiscent of summer camp."

Jack laughed. "You're still shocked about their plans to bring in a sex therapist, aren't you?"

Lynn blushed despite her efforts to keep cool. Somehow she'd known he was going to bring that up. "It just caught me off guard, that's all. If they feel it's needed, then, hey, it's okay with me."

Eyes glimmering, Jack draped his arm on the back of the sofa. "But you couldn't see yourself going to one about any problem?"

"I think I'd try a little one-on-one communication with my partner first."

His eyes darkened. His hand was inches from her shoulder but he made no move to touch her. Still she was as aware of his heat as if he had caressed her skin. "You wouldn't have any qualms expressing yourself?"

Her breath started to quicken. "No, of course not," she said. "Not if I, well, we loved each other."

"And you wouldn't consider making love with a man for any other reason?" He removed his arm from the back of the sofa.

She looked straight at him but was unable to read anything more than curiosity on his face. "No, I wouldn't."

"Me, neither," he said softly. "I learned a long time ago that there's nothing lonelier and emptier than waking up with a complete stranger."

They were getting too close, she thought, and it's happening too fast. And yet she had the sense that maybe this had been fated, that maybe she was a fool to even try and fight it.

"So how many times have you been in love?" Jack asked casually.

"Just once, with my ex-husband."

"Since?"

"I've dated several men, but no one has become important." Until you, she thought helplessly, knowing then it was inevitable. She couldn't stop what she felt for him anymore than she could stop breathing and still live.

His finger traced the curve of her jaw, then stopped, as if sensing her confusion and her need to sort things out. She knew he wouldn't rush her, that he would give her all the time she needed. He looked longingly at her and said, "Let me be that one."

"HI, SORRY I'M LATE," said Lynn after settling into her chair at Valentino's. A popular Italian restaurant, it featured a sumptuous dinner buffet of hot and cold foods, and a decor that included mauve tablecloths and napkins, bentwood chairs and tables.

"I was beginning to think you wouldn't show," Jack said. His glance took in her face, dwelling momentarily on the flushed color in her cheeks and windswept hair.

Lynn tucked a few errant strands into place. She might still have lingering doubts about the wisdom of getting any more involved with him, but she couldn't help appreciate the enamored way he was looking at her. Still, this was just a business meeting. He'd called her because he wanted to talk about the two cases he was interested in and she was simply, as always, taking all the help she could get. She couldn't, wouldn't read more into the invitation to meet him after work than that. "I wouldn't stand you up for dinner," she reassured him with a grin. She wasn't that type of person. "I got hung up with a potential client back at my office."

"Another case?" He signaled the waiter to bring her a menu.

Lynn accepted it with thanks, deciding on a drink and the dinner buffet. Jack ordered the same.

"Did you get the job?"

"No. I turned her down." Lynn's mouth curled derisively. "She didn't want a private investigator, she wanted a dating service." At Jack's questioning look, she explained, "She wanted me to compile a list of the ten richest men in the city for her—with in-depth profiles on all of them. She planned to pay me back when she'd married one of them."

His eyes flashed his amusement. She was glad to see someone thought it was funny! "And you said no?"

Lynn rolled her eyes. "I'm here to solve people's problems, not matchmake. Yes, I said no. I guess I'm old-fashioned, but I still think people should fall in love spontaneously and naturally. Not because some computer has decided you're well suited."

The waiter returned with their drinks and plates. Jack gallantly assisted her with her chair when she rose, and together, they headed for the salad bar. "Unfortunately, falling in love doesn't happen nearly often enough; at least not those affairs with fairy-tale endings," Jack said, helping himself to some lettuce and layering on the mushrooms.

Lynn added tomatoes and cottage cheese to her plate. "Maybe that's life." Who said being alone was necessarily miserable?

"Maybe." Jack sprinkled grated cheese onto his vegetables and reached for the Thousand Island dressing. "In a way I kind of admire people who go after what they want, no-holds-barred. Maybe that's better than just letting life drift along and lamenting what you don't have. For instance," he continued before Lynn could disagree, as they returned to their seats. "I always figured I'd have a family by now. But unlike some people, I haven't gone out and done something about it."

Suddenly, Lynn's throat became unbearably dry. Here it came, the subject she'd hoped would never come up with him—children. "What do you mean?" she asked hoarsely, wishing this discussion didn't remind her so much of the case Lynn had handled for Theresa.

Unaware of the nature of her thoughts, Jack continued, "Some hire surrogates, some adopt or try to have test-tube babies. But one way or another they're working to have their families."

Lynn's heart started pounding and her hands became slippery with perspiration. Determined to get control of herself and her emotions, she wiped her hands on the napkin in her lap and tried to still their trembling. She had to stay calm, for Theresa's sake and her own, pretend that nothing was amiss. Or had ever been investigated. "If you wanted a child, why didn't you go ahead and just marry someone who wanted the same thing?"

"Because, like you, I'm an old-fashioned person, a hopeless romantic. I want to have it all and not settle for less."

She met his gaze with steady eyes, knowing how much hinged on his answer to her next question. "And marrying someone you didn't love—"

"Would be settling," he said firmly, dismissing the idea. "I'd never do that. But, on the other hand, by remaining so unbending I might be denying myself the chance to have children. I know that and it bothers me."

Lynn knew that feeling, too. "I've always wanted a child," she said softly, looking away. But in the past the time had never been right, and now that she was divorced it seemed an even less likely prospect. It wasn't that she was against marriage, it was that her expectations were so high, and she didn't want to settle for less, either.

"You couldn't consider having a child on your own?" Jack asked gently, trying to understand her.

She knew he had noticed the tension in her and misinterpreted it. She fought to keep her voice level. "You mean just go up to someone you've chosen by their genetic traits and say I want to have a child with you?'' she asked incredulously, trying to imagine herself doing such a thing.

He shrugged. ''Crazier things have happened.''

''That's not for me.'' Lynn was sure about that much.

''Artificial insemination, then?''

''No, I—I'd want to know who the father was.''

''Artificial insemination with the candidate of your choice.''

She saw he was teasing, and yet, if there ever was a chance to find out more about how Jack felt on this subject without raising his suspicions, this was it. She took a deep breath, knowing she had to discover why he'd done what he had—donated sperm—and how he felt about it now. ''What about you?'' she asked leading him into a more intimate discussion. ''Would you ever consider adopting a child on your own?''

He shook his head. ''I think a child needs a mother. To be widowed or divorced and cope as best you can is one thing. To go into it deliberately is another.'' Something he obviously didn't approve of. So how would he feel about Theresa?

She pushed the thought from her mind, that wasn't any of her business. Besides, Carter was happy and well adjusted. She'd been around him since birth, and he never once lacked for anything, especially love. It was an odd thought, though, knowing Jack might have more biological children out there somewhere in the world, children he knew nothing about. She wondered how far his generosity extended. Smiling, she posed a hypothetical question.

"Suppose, for instance, one of your colleagues came to you and asked you to father her child? What would you say to that?"

He understood how serious her questions were, that she wanted to know more about him. He apparently wanted that, too. "I'd have to say no, that I couldn't participate in a situation like that," he answered, his eyes on hers. "It's got the potential for too much heartache because I couldn't knowingly participate in the conception of a child and then once the child was born, step back and just relinquish all rights and control. Nor could I marry someone I didn't love." He shrugged. "So it would never work."

Lynn nodded. She had guessed that much about Jack. It was a relief she'd been right, that he would not be likely to romanticize his relationship with Theresa even if he knew about their child. "I've always wondered about men who donate sperm," she said impulsively. "Or women who donate their eggs. How do they live, knowing they might have a child somewhere?" Could she do the same? Somehow she didn't think so, she wasn't that brave or unselfish.

Jack looked away, not saying anything, and she knew even if he wouldn't say so directly that he was thinking about his own experience. "I imagine they don't let themselves think about it," he said quietly. "From a strictly psychological standpoint, it'd be natural to look for traits of themselves in every child they saw on the street for a while, but eventually they'd stop that and put it from their minds. Then they'd probably concentrate only on the nobility of the gesture, their generosity in helping the childless have a child.''

He really did care about people, she thought. "So you don't think, given a chance, that they'd want to know about any children they might have sired?'' Lynn said, reaffirming what she already knew.

"No. It would drive them crazy if they did," he said firmly.

"I guess so," Lynn said quietly.

She thought a few more minutes, then decided to go for broke. "But what would happen if that person somehow, maybe inadvertently even, found out he or she had a child? Has that ever happened to your knowledge?''

Jack shrugged. "I don't know of any specific incident where the rules of confidentiality have been broken. If it did happen," he said, frowning worriedly now that the discussion had taken a theoretical turn, "I don't know how the people would cope. It would be natural, of course, for the father to feel a sense of responsibility. And that in turn would cause a whole host of problems.

He forced a smile and shrugged off his low mood. "At any rate, that would be a very rare circumstance. Every artificial insemination program that I know of guarantees complete anonymity to all donors. It would be very difficult, if not impossible, for a recipient of the program to get that information.''

Unless that person was a lab technician who knew a friend of a friend.

"How did we get off on that tangent?" he asked. "I asked you to meet me here to talk about Uncle Walter and Jessica. Anything new on either?"

Since he was willing to suddenly drop their previous subject, Lynn decided to let it go, too. "I'm making headway on your uncle's case." The only problem was Walter was bound to dislike the direction her investigation was taking. If her assumption proved right, it would be very humiliating for him.

Before Jack could ask for specifics, she abruptly continued, "As for Jessica, nothing earth-shattering has developed. But I have convinced the Montgomerys to let me run ads with Jessica's photos in the papers of all the major cities—like Chicago, Los Angeles, New York, Dallas, Houston. They're offering one-hundred-dollar rewards for any information about Jessica, so—hope to hear something soon. I have a cooperative agreement with an agency in Chicago and they're going to try and find out if maybe she's working there, or has tried to get a job there. But right now, everything still seems like pretty much of a long shot." They were operating blindly on guesses rather than actual information, and that she didn't like.

"You think it'll be a while?"

"I always hope for the best of course, but my past experience tells me it could be weeks or even months."

"There's nothing more we can do here in the city?"

"No, not really."

He looked wistful. To her surprise, he made no effort to hide his sadness from her. "I'd gotten kind of used to seeing and hearing from you a lot,'' he confessed softly.

Lynn had gotten used to seeing him, too. She felt heat steal into her cheeks, and she couldn't seem to drop her eyes from his.

Jack noticed her reaction and grinned, apparently seeing all that was on her mind. Lynn blushed even more, realizing that despite their differences, the chemistry between them made it all too easy for them to fall into each other's arms. Even now she couldn't forget his kisses, the natural way she had responded, the cherished way he made her feel. They were like magnets of opposite poles; it was impossible for them to stay apart.

"I'm sorry if I got too carried away the last time you were at my place. I know I seemed to be pushing you into making a serious commitment, and I realize that it's much too soon for that. But do you think we could be friends for now?''

More than friends, she thought. Easily. Out loud, she heard herself saying calmly, "Yes.''

"I'd like that," he said quietly, his eyes holding hers. "I'd like that a lot.''

THE REST OF THE WEEK passed swiftly. Lynn worked long hours every day, doing background checks on the people involved in the Golden Glow project and trying to establish leads on Jessica. She checked with employment agencies, retail shops, anywhere Jessica might have found work, in state and out. But she came up with nothing. By the time Saturday rolled around, she was ready for a break, hoping that a day off would revitalize her. But even a quiet day at home brought on a renewed burst of frustration. Lynn stared at the empty towel rack in the upstairs bathroom she and Noland shared. She couldn't even finish her laundry without running into a hitch. "Noland, where's that white teddy I left hanging in the bathroom?" she asked.

"I don't know. I didn't touch it," he protested, giving her a bewildered glance as he came to stand beside her in the upstairs hallway outside the bath. "Unless..."

"What?" Lynn demanded impatiently.

"Unless it got mixed up with my workout clothes."

She let out a yell that sent him scurrying down the stairs with her right after him. They made it to the laundry room simultaneously. The washer had already stopped. Noland opened the lid. It took them roughly ten seconds to find the missing garment. What had once been pure glistening white silk with a beautiful delicate trim was now an unevenly dyed light blue.

Lynn stared at the garment then her brother, almost too angry to speak.

"Oh, God, Lynn, I'm sorry. You know I didn't do it on purpose!"

That was true, she knew. But there were times when that didn't help. Times when she wanted just once to be able to hang her stockings up in the bathroom to dry without having to listen to anyone complain.

Times when she wanted not to have to worry about her feminine needs infringing on anyone else. That time would come, of course, as soon as she made enough money to afford her own place again. But that didn't help her right now.

A flush of righteous indignation in her cheeks, Lynn whirled toward the door, the mangled teddy still in her hands. And it was then that she saw her dad standing there with Jack beside him, apparently witnesses to the scene.

"What are you doing here?" she croaked, looking up into Jack's handsome face. Although she hadn't seen him since Wednesday night, he'd been on her mind almost constantly, along with his idea they be friends, that they see each other occasionally on a purely social level.

He looked both wary and compassionate, as if he knew he'd chosen the worst possible time to drop in and was sorry for his poor timing. When he spoke, his voice was calm and casual. "I came by to see if there was anything new on Jessica—"

"No, there isn't."

"Everything all right in here?" her father asked picking up on the continuing tension between the siblings.

"Everything's fine," Lynn said, deciding she'd been embarrassed enough. She stuffed the ruined teddy into the rag bag in the corner and wiped her damp hands on her jeans.

Noland looked at her and didn't say a word. He knew she was still ready to kill him.

Realizing a rescue was needed, her father cleared his throat and intervened. "I just asked Jack here if he wanted to stay for brunch. The ham and eggs are ready."

Lynn forced a smile. "Great." They all headed for the dining room, and although Jack and her father tried to keep up a conversation, brunch was a desultory affair.

"So what's wrong?" Jack asked after the meal was over and Lynn was clearing the table. Her father and Noland had gone out back to begin the yardwork they had planned. "I mean, obviously your teddy was ruined. But it isn't just that, is it? Something more is bothering you."

"Sometimes it gets to me, living here with my brother and Dad. Don't misunderstand me. I love them both dearly, and they love me. But there's just not enough privacy. I'm used to doing things my own way, in my own time, to having a bathroom all to myself. The situation frustrates me. I fall prey to some of the irritations I had when I was growing up."

"Like Noland's casual handling of your things."

She nodded and then heaved an enormous sigh, glad that he did understand and didn't think her a shrew, despite the fact he'd just seen her at her absolute worst.

Jack finished cleaning the counter, then relaxed beside her, his arms folded across his chest, his legs crossed at the ankles. "Sounds like the normal sibling relationship to me."

"Yeah, but I thought we'd grow out of it by now." Lynn pushed her hair out of her face. A drop of water stayed on her cheek. Jack reached up and dried the moisture with his fingertips.

He shook his head. "Never. All you can do is mellow a little bit. Try to take the petty irritations in stride. Of course it doesn't hurt to lose your temper occasionally, kind of clears the air."

"Yeah, well, what I wouldn't give sometimes to live in a totally feminine household," Lynn said wryly, laughing and shaking her head. The sheer ridiculousness of the situation got to her. "Can you believe it? I actually dream of the day when I can hang my stockings wherever I like, for however long I like."

Jack watched her close the dishwasher. When she straightened, his eyes lingered on the open collar of her blouse. "You thinking about getting a place of your own?" His eyes returned to her face.

So they'd have more privacy. Lynn shook her head. Funny how she grew warm in the places where his gaze strayed. "As much as I'd like to," she said huskily, "financially it's just not feasible until I get my business going. And the petty irritations aside, I really do like being with my family. I just get crazy sometimes." She sighed, glad he seemed to understand she wasn't that grumpy all the time.

"Don't we all," Jack said with a grin, turning to face her. He was just inches away. He seemed to understand her intuitively. He wanted to help her, to soothe. And she wanted that, too.

And then he was touching her. She melted into him, loving his strength, the easy way his lips moved over hers. His fingers tightened on her shoulders, then moved up to slip through her hair. Her lips parted willingly, absorbing the pressure, taking all he had to give, and returning it tenfold. She arched closer, feeling a delicious need pour through her. No one had ever made her feel this wanted. No one had ever roused such strong emotions in her. She desired him body and soul. Heat seeped through her body, and a wanton, delicious ache spread through her body.

The back door creaked open.

Startled, they jerked apart. Her heart still racing, she had never been more aware of Jack than at the moment. She knew it was only a matter of time before they made love. And she wanted that more than she'd ever have thought possible.

Apparently unaware he had interrupted anything, Noland stuck his head inside. "Hey, is it safe to come in yet?" He looked cold.

Lynn took pity on her brother. "Only if you apologize," she said curtly, deciding it was now or never to take a stand with him. He might be older, he might be sweet, but he was too careless sometimes and it was time that changed!

"I'll do better than that," Noland said easily, tromping all the way into the kitchen. "I'll buy you a new one. Exact same size, color, style, everything. Just tell me where you got it."

Lynn had to admit that was more than fair.

"Feeling better now?" Jack asked, when they'd finished the dishes and Noland had departed to get Lynn a new teddy.

"Yes," she admitted sheepishly. She was still a little embarrassed Jack had seen her fight with her brother. Then again, maybe he should know the worst now before they got involved any deeper, although her display of temper didn't seem to bother him.

"Good enough to go with me to the Annual Covered Bridge Festival?"

"Where?" Lynn was intrigued, as well as aware he was more or less asking her for a date. It thrilled her to know that he wanted to be with her.

"It's in Rockville, about an hour's drive from here," he answered casually, shoving his hands into his pockets. "They've got thirty-four covered bridges on five specific routes. There are tour buses, but I prefer to get a color-coded map and drive it myself because it gives me a chance to view the bridges at a more leisurely pace." It was clear they'd do whatever she wanted.

Lynn smiled, warming to his thoughtfulness. "I didn't know you were interested in anything like this." It was a new side of him, one she liked very much.

He grinned, looking both sheepish and pleased with himself. "Now that I take time out to stop and smell the roses, I find there's a lot to see," he said, then proceeded to name a few. "The street artists in Tangier, the old-fashioned soda fountain in Marshall, the quilts at Gobbler's Knob Country Store. In Rockville they have a lot of different booths. We can browse there, too."

"Sounds fun." She smiled, finding a day out was just what she needed. Lately she'd had too much frustration, work and worry in her life, and not enough play.

Chapter Eight

Lynn was feeling remarkably content as she and Jack surveyed a particularly beautiful double span bridge over Sugar Creek. The longest bridge in Parke County, it was 315 feet long. It was a retired bridge, which meant it was walkable but closed to traffic.

The day was beautiful, the country atmosphere serene. The leaves on the trees were shades of gold, rust and red. Birds sang. They were alone as they strolled hand in hand through the shadowy interior of the long and narrow red wooden bridge. "It's hard to believe this has been here since 1876," Jack murmured, looking up at the high-placed gaps in the wood that served as windows.

Lynn shivered in the cool autumn air. "Enduring, isn't it? Gives one a sense of history."

"And occasionally the shivers," he said, laughing and drawing her near. His arm around her warmed her. "Sure you aren't still spooked by the Sim Smith Bridge?" he teased.

Lynn shivered again, remembering the bridge's shadowy interior, imagining how spooky it might be at night, particularly if you knew it was supposed to be haunted by the ghost of an Indian squaw who carried her papoose across it. "And all those scarecrows around didn't help." They had seemed to be everywhere, particularly where she least expected to see them.

"Those scarecrows are for the scarecrow contest," he laughed, knowing how startled she'd been when she stumbled upon the first one, a grotesque caricature of the Grim Reaper.

"Yes, well, I don't know how many crows have been driven off, but that last one—the witch—sure scared me."

Jack tightened his hand over hers. "I kind of liked the exhibit that had Ma and Pa fighting over his drinking, although I must say that cast iron frying pan she was about to hit him with looked as if it would hurt." He rubbed his head, imagining the pain.

"Good reason to give up the corn liquor." They came to the end of the bridge, and Lynn paused. She couldn't remember when she'd had such a good time or enjoyed being with someone more. He looked as if he was feeling the same. "Thanks for asking me to come with you, today," she said softly. "I really am having fun." It was exactly the break she had needed.

"I'm having fun, too. In fact, this is my idea of heaven—quiet time in a natural setting alone with a beautiful woman." He drew her nearer. "But not just any beautiful woman," he amended softly. "Just you."

His mouth descended to hers, and he put everything he felt into that single heated caress. He gave and he took, asking not for surrender, but possession—mutual possession.

Impossible as it seemed, she had forgotten the way it felt to be kissed thoroughly, and held on to him as though she might faint, as though she never wanted him to stop. Or maybe she had never known how wonderful and gratifying mere kissing could be. Was this love? she wondered whimsically. And if it wasn't, was there anything more beautiful, more spectacular?"

"You look . . . wistful," he said softly, still holding her close after the kiss had drawn to an end.

She *was* wistful. Savoring their privacy—the momentary lack of other tourists in the area—she leaned her head against his shoulder, soaking in his warmth. If only she could tell him all that was in her heart and mind, so they could start again with a clean slate, with nothing between them. But she couldn't. The best she could do was to forget she had ever investigated him for Theresa. "I want everything to be simple," she murmured. She wanted no conflicts of interest in her relationship with him, no arguments about her job, and how he thought she should do it, nothing but the here and now.

"Life is never simple," he said softly, stroking first her hair, then her cheek.

"Yes, but . . ." It could be easier.

Mistaking the reason behind her apprehension, he said softly, "I know how it is for everyone after a divorce. You're feeling a little wary. I understand, Lynn, and I've promised not to rush you." He took a deep, shaky breath. "And I'm trying." But he wanted more.

She lifted her face to his. She saw the glowing love in his eyes and they exchanged tentative smiles. And suddenly she knew everything was going to be all right. Somehow, someway, they would work out any problems that came up. There was beginning to be too much at stake for them not to do so.

Relaxing slightly, too, he released his hold on her and glanced at the brochure in his hands. "We've got plenty more sights to see. I guess we'd better get going." In the distance a tour bus loomed.

Lynn nodded. "I guess we'd better."

Five o'clock that night found them wandering down the main street of Rockville. Having seen most of the sights, they'd decided on a dinner break. Beneath a huge tent were eighty stalls filled with a variety of arts and crafts for sale. In one, Jack saw hand-knitted caps and mittens, emblazoned with the festival logo. Catching his yearning look at the children's apparel, she teased, "Jack, they're too small."

"Yeah, I know—"

"But you still want one."

"Actually," he said, taking her hand in his and moving on toward the next booth, "I'd like to have a sweater."

"Mmmm, I don't think I've seen any here tonight."

"No, and you probably won't. I haven't had one since I was a kid. My mother used to knit me sweaters. I used to hate them, too."

Lynn paused to admire an assortment of hand-made birdhouses in the next booth. "Did she make you wear them anyway?" All the clerks in the festival were dressed as they would have been a century before—the women in long calico dresses, aprons and bonnets or caps, the men in hand-tailored suits and string ties, or pants with suspenders.

"Oh, yeah," Jack continued, walking over to a booth where homemade apple butter and corn cob jelly were displayed. "You bet she made me wear those sweaters." He grinned, reminiscing, then added, "It wasn't until I was much older, when I was taking my first college psych class, a basic introductory course, and had to do a paper on parent-child relationships that I realized how loved and cherished I felt whenever I'd worn those sweaters. Strange as it may sound, that was the beginning of my knowing I wanted to be a psychiatrist. I was intrigued by the difference something little like that could make in a child's life. I wondered what happened to kids who grew up without love. Or understanding."

"Were your parents surprised by your choice of profession?"

"My dad was."

"What about your mom?"

"Mom understood. But then she's always had a knack for understanding people, kind of sensing what they needed. When I was a kid, she used to open up her kitchen to anyone who had a problem. Women, children, people from church, they used to come in and just pour their hearts out to my mom. Sometimes she'd give them advice, sometimes she'd just listen. It didn't really seem to matter. Just knowing she was there for them made a difference. And people always left feeling better. I've tried to do that for my patients."

"I'm sure you do," Lynn said impulsively. "You do that for me and I'm not even—"

He grinned, pleased. "Well, that's good to know." He took her hand and clasped it firmly in his. For a long time, they strolled, looking at everything. Spying something of particular interest, Jack pointed to a booth at the far end of the tent. "There's an old-time photographer's booth. Want to have your picture taken?"

"Sounds like fun." It'd be a lasting reminder of this wonderful day.

Minutes later, they were poring over the choice of costumes. They finally decided on the gunslinger and the saloon girl. They retired to separate booths to change, and returned to the main area. Lynn stared at Jack. In white shirt, black pants, black jacket and black string tie, a black Stetson slanted rakishly low over one brow, he looked mesmerizingly handsome. And faintly dangerous. In contrast, she felt, well, just a tiny bit wicked. The gold and red saloon girl's costume had a low-cut bodice, and it clung to her figure provocatively. She wore feathers in her hair, a black garter and fishnet stockings on her legs.

Seeing her, he gave a low whistle. "If I'd have known you were gonna look like that," he whispered in her ear, "I'd have hustled you over here a lot sooner."

Lynn's heart was racing. "You look pretty terrific yourself," she whispered back, suddenly very conscious of how much she wanted to make love with him. She was thankful when the photographer interrupted them with directions on how to pose for the picture.

Back in street clothes, they ventured out onto the courthouse square. Food booths sent out tempting aromas. Discovering they were hungry, they ate some of the American Legion's barbecued chicken, the Little League's baked potatoes, the Jaycees' corn on the cob and finished it off with pink lemonade and sugar cookies from Rowe and Chaney.

"Well, only one more bridge route to see," Jack said, studying the map. "We could do that, although it'll be dark by the time we get there. Or we could go to the theater and see the play the chamber of commerce is sponsoring. Your choice."

At that point, she felt up for everything. She'd spent almost eight hours with him, and yet she felt reluctant to part company. This was new for Lynn, this sensation of never wanting to be without him.

"I opt for the bridge."

Jack grinned. "My choice, too."

In silence, they drove to the Narrows Bridge in Turkey Run State Park. Jack got out of the car. "I saved this for last," he said, taking her hand, "because it's supposed to be one of the most scenic spots in the county."

Built high above the water, the double-span red and white bridge was beautiful in the moonlight. "It's so peaceful out here," Lynn said.

They walked down the path to the embankment to look at the gently flowing waters of Sugar Creek. The shallow water glistened in the moonlight. The night air was cool and still. Above, the black velvet sky glittered with a thousand stars. She felt utterly alone with him, utterly safe and content. "I want you to know something. This has been the nicest day I've had in a long time," he said, turning her to him.

"For me, too," she agreed. Then without warning, his mouth lowered until it was on hers. He was kissing her as if he never wanted to stop, and she was kissing him back just as ardently, showing him all she felt for him. When they drew apart long moments later, both were trembling. Lynn was weak-kneed, dizzy. Hands on his forearms, she clung to him for heart-stopping moments. This was real, what she was feeling. It was undeniable. He knew it, too. She was in over her head now, and liking it.

He pulled away for a moment and looked deeply into her eyes. Seeing her approval there, he put a hand beneath her chin, lifted her face to his and kissed her again, long and hard and deep, until she was gasping for breath. Then he kissed her gently, a kiss full of tenderness. "I want you in my life," he said softly before he let her go. "I want you all the time."

Lynn knew exactly how he felt. Because despite the complications, she felt exactly the same.

LYNN STAGGERED NUMBLY out of her office late Monday evening, her feelings of frustration acute and heartfelt. She'd been on the phone most of the day, tracking down all possible leads on Jessica, following up on the newspaper ads the family had placed. Again, her efforts had left her with zilch. And none of the other agencies whom she had cooperative agreements with had come up with anything, either. Right now she didn't know if she would ever find Jessica. She wondered how she would tell Mary Montgomery if she couldn't find her; the gentle woman was counting on Lynn to succeed.

To make matters worse, her investigation into Golden Glow was uncovering more and more information that hinted at dishonest behavior. It thrilled her to think that she was on to something, but at the same time she hoped her intuition was wrong. She didn't relish the idea of being the one to dash Walter's retirement paradise.

"Lynn, sweetheart, is that you?" her father called from the other room, above the sounds of Monday-night football.

"Yeah."

"Through for the night?" her father asked.

"Yeah. I've done all I can do." Lynn shouted back, then glass of beer and bowl of popcorn in hand, she walked back into the room to join her brother and father. She stopped dead in the entryway, amazed to see Jack settled in an easy chair watching the game.

Her tongue refused to function for several seconds. She felt joy and disquiet. "I didn't know you were here," she said finally.

Jack stood. "I stopped by earlier to see if you wanted to go to a movie or something with me, but Noland told me you were still working—"

"And Jack didn't want to disturb you," Noland cut in, helping himself to some more popcorn. "So I asked him to watch the game with us."

"I hope you don't mind." Jack gave her a courteous glance, letting her know he respected her work and its importance, even if he didn't always like the way she went about her sleuthing.

"No, of course not," Lynn said, wishing she felt a little less awkward and caught off guard, and that her brother and father would vanish. The truth was she was glad to see Jack. Very glad. She just wished she'd had a little warning and time to run a brush through her hair or put a little lipstick on. Instead, she was wearing jeans and an old sweatshirt whereas Jack was dressed to go out—in a navy sweater and slacks that brought out the blue of his eyes. As always, he was ruggedly handsome, his dark hair shining and well brushed, his jaw clean-shaven.

Noticing her prolonged scrutiny of him, his mouth curved up in a slow, sensual smile. She felt the impact of his look all the way to her knees.

"Well, the game's about over." Her father yawned exaggeratedly, picking up on the tension in the room and Lynn's desire to be alone with her beau. "I guess I'll watch the rest of it upstairs." He stood and gave Noland a nudge.

Lynn silently blessed her father's perceptiveness. "Uh, me, too." Noland got hastily to his feet. He gave his sister a telling look, one that said he knew full well what was on her mind, and held her—not Jack—responsible. "Uh, behave yourselves, you guys." He started up the stairs, stopped midway and came back down, heading for the front door. Noting it was nearly eleven, Lynn asked curiously, "Hey, where are you going?"

"Out for a carton of milk. I forgot we were almost out and I promised Dad I'd pick some up earlier."

Noland looked tired suddenly; his pending divorce plus his work as a cop were wearing him out. Lynn exchanged a glance with Jack; he seemed amenable to whatever she wanted. "Do you want us to go?" she asked Noland. "I wouldn't mind."

Noland shook his head. "No, that's okay. You guys sit tight and enjoy yourselves. "I'm just going to run down to the convenience store on the corner. I'll be right back." He started out the door, then came back, and unable to resist, delivered his parting shot. "Don't worry, sis. I won't interrupt."

Getting his message loud and clear, Lynn aimed a throw pillow at his head.

He ducked out, laughing.

Lynn sat in a corner of the sofa. Jack turned the sound down on the television to a barely audible murmur. "You don't mind me showing up here, do you? I tried to call, but your line was busy."

"No, I don't mind." She welcomed his visits and cherished the time they shared. "There wasn't anything wrong, was there?"

"Besides the fact I was lonely?"

She blushed. "I'm serious."

"So am I. I get very lonely without you, Lynn. I think about you all the time."

"I think about you, too," she said softly.

Warmth flooded her at his nearness. He seemed suddenly vulnerable to her and very relaxed at the same time, as if he felt at home there.

He leaned forward and helped himself to more popcorn. "So," he said lazily, checking out the instant replay on the screen. "Get all your work done?"

"No." Lynn shook her head. "I'm still working on a missing persons case."

She didn't specify, but Jack knew which one. "Any luck?" He seemed to wish she had been successful.

Again, Lynn shook her head. She closed her eyes briefly and slouching down, rested her head on the back of the sofa. God, she was tired, physically exhausted and emotionally wrung out. "No, none." She yawned and rubbed a hand over her eyes. "Times like this, I want to just give up. But I know I can't. I have to keep trying. Nothing beats the satisfaction of reuniting a family. I have to keep believing that it'll happen, that we'll all get a happy ending."

"And if you don't get a happy ending, will you be able to hack it?" Jack moved closer. He stretched his long legs out next to hers, so they were touching from hip to toe. She felt his body heat and the bunched muscles in his legs. She sucked in her breath, incredibly moved by his slightest touch.

Aware he was waiting for an answer, she concentrated on his question. Lynn shrugged, refusing to let herself dwell on negative possibilities; they were too draining. "If I've done everything possible, yeah, I can handle it," she said. Fortunately, since she'd been a private investigator and able to pull out all the stops to find a solution, she hadn't had to deal with many unhappy endings.

"Can I ask you something else?" He reached over and twined hands with her, tracing gentle patterns on her skin.

"Sure."

"Do you ever sense you're getting too personally involved in your cases, too caught up in your work?"

She heard the hesitation in his voice, the concern. "All the time," she said softly. She sighed, knowing he was right, that sometimes she did work too hard and too long. "But it's not something I can help. The nature of my business and all that." She had to follow the trail while the trail existed. The fact that she was subcontracting detectives from Chicago agencies to help her accomplish the legwork faster made her involvement no less important. Every day, she checked up on leads and plotted out new strategies.

Jack opened his mouth to say something else, but just then two things happened—Dallas scored and the phone rang. Lynn reached over and picked up the receiver, watching with amusement as Jack moaned and groaned and muttered at the people on television. "Hello," she said, the smile still in her voice.

The voice on the end of the line was unfamiliar—and grim. A prickle of alarm went through her. It intensified unremittingly until her whole body was chilled to the bone. Shaking, she listened for several more seconds, feeling the blood drain from her face, and a sense of unreality pervade her. *No,* she thought. *This isn't happening. Not again.*

Everything around her slipped into slow motion; it was as if reality were a movie projector on the blink, interspersing her view of the living room with other pictures—pictures she didn't want to see. And she was an unwilling watcher of what was going on.

"What is it? Lynn? What's wrong?" Jack's voice came to her, a great distance away.

"It's Noland," she heard herself say in a thin, reedy voice. "We have to get Dad and go to the hospital. Oh, God, Jack—" she started to cry as she buried her face in his shoulder "—Noland's been shot."

Chapter Nine

"Can I get you a cup of coffee?" Jack asked solicitously.

"No, nothing." Lynn paced the waiting room, her arms hugged tight to her chest. Farther down the hallway, standing just outside the surgery doors, were her father and Noland's estranged wife, Gail. Of petite stature, she was impeccably groomed, even at that hour of night, wearing a soft wool skirt, blouse, and matching cardigan. Gail had always been ultraconservative, extremely efficient and well organized. She was by nature a planner, but she hadn't planned for this, and her eyes were red and puffy from crying. And yet, somehow, she was calm, too.

"Gail and your father both seem to be holding up fairly well," Jack said softly, glancing over at the slender red-haired woman who would soon be divorced from Noland.

Lynn shrugged, feeling angry and restless. She wanted to strike out at something, anything. She wanted to vent some of this rage she was feeling. This shouldn't have happened to Noland! He didn't deserve this, not after all he had been through this year.

Needing to get her mind on something other than the injustices of fate, Lynn looked over at her father. Yes, he was doing fine. Always steady and never more so than when in a crisis. He hadn't cried, hadn't sworn, hadn't said much of anything except to ask the doctors if his son would be all right. And when they said they couldn't guarantee anything until after surgery, Sid just turned whiter. Lynn envied her dad and his ability to control his emotions whenever necessary. She couldn't do that. She always felt something—whether it was guilt or joy or sorrow—even when she didn't want to admit it. And she'd never been more emotional than when dealing with her brother. They had always tormented and infuriated each other and been one another's staunchest friends.

Without warning, she heard herself talking, telling Jack what was on her mind. "Yes, well, I guess we are all holding up, as you say, but then maybe that's not surprising." Bitterness colored her low tone. Tears stung her eyes and tightened her throat. "This isn't the first time Noland's been badly hurt," she said hoarsely. "He was shot once before, while on duty."

"How? What happened?"

"He went into a bar to break up a fight and one of the men pulled a gun. We didn't think he'd live that time." Lynn's voice cracked. Jack put an arm around her and she leaned against him, feeling the tears spill heedlessly down her face. Her shoulders shook with the effort it took to hold back the sobs.

"He's going to be all right, Lynn." Jack's voice and touch were strong and sure.

"I know that," she said in a wavering voice. She wouldn't let herself believe anything else. But right now it all seemed like a nightmare. Noland leaving and the call minutes later telling her there'd been a robbery at the convenience store and that Noland had been shot in the chest while subduing the suspect.

Realizing how close she was to collapsing, Jack guided her to the vinyl sofa. He sat down beside her, and putting an arm around her shoulders, hugged her close. He clasped her right hand in his left. "Tell me about Gail and Noland," he said in a low, commanding tone.

"They're getting divorced."

"I know that. Why?"

"She hated his work." Lynn took a tissue from her pocket, dried her eyes and blew her nose. "She couldn't stand the stress of being married to a cop and never knowing if he was going to come home at night. She wanted him to do something safer—take a desk job, or change jobs completely. He wouldn't."

Jack was silent, taking that in. He looked down the hall to where Gail was standing with Lynn's dad. "Is that what happened to your marriage, too?"

It was a curious question, but she knew he was just trying to get her talking to pass the time. "No," she said wearily, unable to hold back an involuntary shiver. Since the phone call, it seemed, she hadn't been able to stop shaking. "Robert didn't mind the danger. He felt life was a crap shoot anyway. He left me because he felt I betrayed him.''

Jack got up and returned with her coat. Lynn leaned forward, and he put it over her shoulders. He took his jacket and draped it over her knees. She still couldn't stop shaking, but the extra clothing helped.

"Betrayed him how?" Jack asked, putting his arm around her again.

She leaned into his protective embrace, feeling very glad he was there for her. Her teeth chattered slightly while she explained. "While I was on the police force, there was an indication that we had an inside leak. We had been investigating an alleged bribery and kick-back scam between city officials making new zoning laws and the local builders, real estate brokers and some salespeople.''

"So?"

"Evidence had indicated Robert was using me and my knowledge of the investigation to allow the criminals to stay one step ahead of the force. Because I had easiest access, I was assigned the task of investigating my husband's real-estate firm.''

"And you did it?" His expression was bland.

"I had to, it was my job.''

"You could have refused."

"I felt I had to do what was asked of me. Besides," she continued defensively, remembering what a tough time that had been for her, "I wanted to know the truth." This revelation upset him, she could see it in his eyes. Lynn paused, searching for a way to explain this, so he would understand she'd done what she did not out of choice but because she was trapped, because there was no other recourse for her. "In the end, I couldn't trust it to anyone else. You have to understand, I never for one moment wanted to believe Robert was guilty. I wanted him to be innocent more badly than you could ever know."

Jack still looked disapproving and troubled by what she had done. "Was he guilty?"

Lynn looked down the hall. Her father and Gail were pacing. There was no word from the surgery department yet. "No, but some of Robert's friends were. And so was my boss. He was fired and charged accordingly."

"All's well that end's well?" Jack finished his own cup of coffee. His mouth was grim as the last bitter dregs went down his throat.

"Not quite," Lynn said candidly, her thoughts drifting back to that ugly, hurtful time. With her fingers, she pleated the fabric of the jacket on her lap. "When the story broke in the papers, Robert knew what I'd done. He was furious that I had lied and deceived him for the three months of the investigation. He said he didn't even know me. He felt betrayed." And his attitude, in turn, had made Lynn angry. His refusal to even try and see things from her point of view still rankled. She swallowed hard, continuing, "In the end, Robert just couldn't accept my not telling him, even though I couldn't." She threw off the two coats and got up, suddenly needing to walk around. "I would have understood had the situation been reversed."

Jack's glance narrowed; he wasn't sure he could say the same thing. "Was there nothing else you could've done?"

Lynn shrugged, wishing they'd never started this discussion, but knowing now that they had, they had to finish it. "We already knew there was a leak in the department." She walked over to the window and stared out at the night. Five in the morning, there was still very little traffic. She turned back to Jack, her arms crossed at her waist, her posture defensive. His attitude was too reminiscent of Robert's. She didn't like his faintly accusing tone or the fact that even his mild disapproval hurt. She'd thought she was through with having other people judge her.

With effort, she kept her voice level. "Suppose I had handed this over to someone else in the department, someone not clever enough to figure out, as I eventually did, that Robert and I both were being set up to take the rap by my boss? What then? Robert and I might both have ended up in jail!"

She had done the only thing she could, and her clever work had kept her ex-husband out of jail! But had he been grateful to her? No! Instead, he'd acted as if she were another Benedict Arnold.

"Robert didn't appreciate your undercover work, the fact that in the end you proved his innocence."

"No," she said bitterly. "To him, it was black and white. I had lied to him and he couldn't forgive me. I couldn't forgive him for being so stubborn and narrow-minded. That being the case, there was only one thing for us to do—divorce. Which we did. I haven't looked back since.''

Jack was quiet. He remained motionless for several minutes, thinking about all she'd said. Lynn could see he wanted to understand her and what she'd done. He was also interested in the reasons for the break-up of her marriage, but that was to be expected. She'd certainly inquired about his divorce.

He fastened a penetrating gaze on her face. ''Was that the only thing wrong with your marriage?''

Leave it to a psychiatrist to ask all the pertinent questions. Leave it to her to not want to answer. Lynn was silent, collecting her thoughts. ''Maybe not,'' she said finally, glad he'd help her find insight into the past. ''I guess if we'd truly communicated, it never would have come to that, to my investigating him behind his back. I mean, if he'd really loved me, wouldn't he have known there was something wrong? Wouldn't he have sensed I was under pressure? Instead, the whole time I was conducting the investigation, he never guessed.'' And Lynn had to admit, in retrospect, it hadn't been because she was such a great actor; in fact, she'd been a lousy sleuth. She was moody around her husband because she wanted him to pick up on the abnormality, wanted him to demand to know what was wrong. Only he didn't notice. And that was a betrayal in itself, the fact that she was going through sheer hell, and her husband didn't have a clue. He didn't care until later when it came to the matter of *his* pride.

Jack walked over to the window and stood next to her, watching as the first pale streaks of dawn lit up the sky. "Ten to one, Lynn," he said softly, "your husband loved you."

"Maybe. And maybe not." She felt irritable now, she didn't know why.

"He couldn't be expected to read your mind."

"Why not? You can." She didn't mean to say them, the words just slipped out.

Jack smiled. "Maybe you were just too good a cop," he said softly. "Good enough to fool Robert."

Lynn held Jack's gaze, knowing they were talking about much more than her past marriage. "And maybe the intimacy we should have had was never there to begin with."

Jack was silent, understanding. His voice turned to a low, soothing pitch, one that probably worked miracles on ladies in distress. "I'm sorry. That must have been a bad time for you."

So bad Lynn didn't even want to think about it. The fights, the screaming, the coldness. "It was." She paused reflectively and took a deep breath. "But some good came out of it, too." She tipped her face up to Jack's. "I realized as time went on that in my efforts to prove myself a good strong cop I'd let myself become too immersed in my work.

"By the time the investigation ended, I didn't like myself or my work very much. I knew I couldn't go on as I had, and that I couldn't survive in the department unless I did go on exactly that same way. As a detective, it was expected of me. I had to do whatever work I was assigned, however they thought best. I wanted to choose my cases, spend more time on helping people—rather than building cases against them.''

Approval in his voice, Jack queried softly, ''Do you like being a private investigator more than a cop?''

Lynn nodded. ''I haven't been in business very long, but yes, I do. It's nice not having to rely on written rules of conduct so much and being able to go on my own determination of what's right and wrong and follow my gut instincts more.''

His shoulders were stiff, his whole body motionless. ''What do you mean?''

Although he tried to keep it out, she heard the faint note of disapproval in his voice, and remembered what he'd said about his ex-wife—that she'd been a social worker who'd never known where or how to draw the line.

''The one thing I've learned over the past ten years is that the same rules don't always apply to every situation, that life isn't as black and white as we would like it to be.'' Sometimes hard choices have to be made.

''And when it isn't?'' Was it her imagination or was there an unsympathetic note in his voice?

''Then I wing it.'' He glanced away, restlessly moved across the room, his strides long and slow. Lynn followed him. It was important he understood this much about her, about how she worked. And there was no time like the present for clearing up misunderstandings. ''Take me talking to your secretary about Jessica. I know that's unethical.'' She held up a hand, preventing his interruption. "But I'd tried all the usual routes to no avail. That one off-the-cuff conversation helped me discover that Jessica is a girl who knows what she's doing, or at least seems to. It helped me decide which way to try and trace her."

She saw the confusion on his face, anger, because he disapproved of any tampering with ethical questions, and understanding, because he knew her motivations were noble and that he wanted to find Jessica, too. "I need you to understand that I do what I have to, no more, no less," she said softly. "I need you to accept my line of work completely."

"And if I can't sometimes? What then?"

"It'll never work for us if you try and judge me or stop me from doing what I have to do."

At her response, he stiffened even more and looked at her contemptuously. Seeing his reaction, something hot backed up in her throat.

"That sounds like an ultimatum," he said quietly, his eyes holding hers in a penetrating stare.

"Maybe it is."

Silence.

Avoiding her glance, he strode to the window and stood looking out for a long time. Lynn was silent, knowing he needed time to assimilate all she'd told him. He turned back to face her, his tone and expression careful. "If it happened again, if you were asked to investigate the man you loved, would you do it?"

She didn't even have to think about that; the one episode in her life had been terrible enough. Lynn shook her head. "No. I never want to be in that position again. If it happened, I'd step back and find someone else to do it." She was sorry she'd ever investigated Jack, but that had happened before she'd gotten to know him, and there was nothing she could do to erase that.

Just then the surgery doors swung open and the surgeon walked out. His clothes were drenched with perspiration. Jack and Lynn moved toward him, as did her father and Gail. "The next twenty-four hours are going to be crucial, but I think Noland's going to make it," the surgeon said.

Gail's lower lip trembled. "Will there by any permanent damage?"

"We're hoping not. The bullet just missed his lung. You'll be able to see him in the morning."

Gail looked at the family, then back at the surgeon. Her green eyes were watery with tears. *She still loves him,* Lynn thought, *with all her heart and soul. It's wrong for them to be getting divorced.*

"I'm staying," Gail said quietly, her determination to be with Noland evident. To the rest of the family she suggested, "Why don't you all go on home and get some rest? We can trade places later."

"Come on. I'll drive," Jack volunteered. Reluctantly, Lynn and her dad agreed, realizing it was best they got some rest now so they could take turns spelling each other later that day.

Once out of the hospital, relief and hope streamed through Lynn. Maybe there was a reason for this after all. Wouldn't it be wonderful if Gail and Noland got back together?

PREDICTABLY the next few days were rough. Gail was at the hospital as much as Lynn and her father combined. Only when Noland came out of intensive care and was moved to a private room did she go back to her normal routine. Lynn knew how much it had cost Gail to become involved in Noland's life again, after working so hard to distance herself from the family. And the first time they had a few moments alone, she told her so.

"Thanks for being here for Noland," Lynn said as they approached the hospital snack bar.

Gail's complexion took on a waxy hue as she pulled a soda can from a vending machine and sat down at a nearby table. She flipped open the top, took a long drink, and then reached for the yarn and needles in her bag. Her motions were quick and jerky as she began to knit. "Don't make too much of this—"

"He has."

Gail looked up, correcting kindly, "No. Noland understands." She paused, seeing Lynn didn't. "I still care abut him very much, but we're getting divorced, Lynn."

Was that all it was? Lynn wondered as she got herself a drink and sat down opposite Gail. Was it just simple friendship between Noland and Gail? Or was there more to it than that, even if Gail didn't want to acknowledge it now that the crisis was over?

But Gail wouldn't talk about her marriage anymore, and she switched the subject abruptly. "So what's all this between you and that hunk Jack Taggart? How did that come about?"

Lynn didn't want to remember. She took a drink of her juice and tried to erase the sudden dryness in her voice. "I met him while passing out flyers on my business. Our, uh, friendship kind of developed from there." Feeling awkward, she glanced around the room, her eyes lighting on the sandwich machine across from her.

"Is that all it is?" Gail asked, her eyes wide. "Friendship?"

Lynn grinned, deciding payback was fair. "I ought to be asking you the same thing." She used her best matchmaking tone.

"No, you shouldn't," Gail's lips pressed together, before she teased back lightly, "and I asked first."

Lynn sighed, knowing if she didn't tell all, Gail would never give up. They had been like real sisters to each other, not just in-laws. Since the separation, she had missed seeing Gail often, but she'd also had sense enough to know Gail needed some time apart, and Lynn had tried to give it to her.

"I'm attracted to him," Lynn said finally, trying to describe her relationship to Jack in five words or less.

Gail grinned, her eyes still on her knitting. "And that's all?"

No, that wasn't all, Lynn was crazy about him. The trouble was she couldn't decide if she was a fool for even entertaining the idea of falling in love with him, especially when she knew how ambivalent his feelings were about her work. Yes, he appreciated her efforts to find Jessica, and depended on her to accomplish that feat, but he didn't always like her methods. And she sensed that wouldn't change.

On the other hand, he wasn't averse to talking about it, trying to work things through, and that was something Robert had never been willing to do. She just had to keep an open mind, she decided. Jack, too. And then everything would work out, she was sure of it.

Having cheered herself up, Lynn looked down at the half-finished garment in Gail's hand. "What are you knitting?"

"A dress. Why? Don't tell me you finally want to learn?" In the past, Gail had unsuccessfully tried to get Lynn to take up knitting as a hobby.

Lynn had always eschewed such time-consuming crafts, complaining needlework gave her a tremendous headache. But she couldn't get Jack's feelings about the sweaters his mother had knitted him out of her mind. Christmas was also coming up, and she needed to get presents. Should she make them this year? Her dad would probably love a hand-knitted sweater, not to mention Noland...and...

Lynn took a second look at Gail's flying fingers. Suddenly, knitting didn't look all that hard. Or headache producing. "Remember all those times you offered to teach me how to knit?"

Gail smiled and nodded.

Lynn laughed. "Well, I'm taking you up on it. Right now."

Chapter Ten

"Jack, you had a call while you were over at the hospital." Andrea handed him the message as soon as he walked in the office door. "From Jessica Montgomery."

His secretary's words hit him like a blast of unexpectedly cold air. Jack stopped short in his tracks. "Did she leave a message?" he asked casually, keeping his face expressionless.

Andrea shook her head worriedly. "No. I asked her if she wanted to leave one, but she said no. She'd try and get you some other time."

Which meant she still didn't want to be found. Jack was aware his heartbeat had picked up. "Was the call of a professional nature?" He hoped nothing was wrong.

"She said no. In fact, she made it crystal clear that she didn't want your help professionally this time. She said she just wanted to talk to you, 'friend to friend.'"

"Did she leave a number where I could reach her?"

"No. I suggested it of course, but she refused. She hung up pretty quickly after that, too."

"How'd she sound?"

"Depressed. Troubled. I'm sorry—I did the best I could."

"It's all right," Jack soothed. "If it's important, she'll call back." He knew that if there was one thing Jessica was not shy about, it was asking for help when she felt she needed it.

"What are you going to do?" Andrea asked.

"I'm not sure. I don't know what I can do." Jack frowned. Jessica was legally of age to live her life the way she wanted. And yet he knew how worried her parents were, and that they had reason to be fearful about her welfare because Jessica wasn't acting in the most laudable manner. But as for what he should do next, he didn't know. One thing was certain—he hated being caught in the middle of this family mess.

"There was something else," Andrea said, interrupting his thoughts. "The call was collect."

"Money trouble," Jack concluded out loud.

Andrea's eyes widened. "That's what I thought, too."

"Did it sound like she was calling from a pay phone?"

"Yeah, it did. I could hear a lot of people talking in the background."

"Any announcements for planes or buses?"

"No. It just sounded like there were a lot of people in the background."

Damn, Jack thought, that could be any public place. He wondered what had prompted Jessica to call him again after all this time. Was she traveling once

more, checking in with "home" between planes? He'd
thought when she left his office after their last session
that he would never hear from her again. Of course,
he hadn't known then she also planned on leaving
town and that he would get involved in finding her. He
understood why she felt she had to go. In some ways
it was a positive step for her. But he wished she had
acted more openly, telling others where she could be
reached and what she was doing. But again, he knew
in her situation that may not have been possible. Certainly her parents, determined and single-minded,
would have done everything to stop her and keep her
home.

After due consideration, he decided the call was a
positive sign. Even if she was upset, at least she was
reaching out again. The question was, he realized, beginning to get the knack of this sleuthing business,
from how far away was she reaching?

Jack saw patients the rest of the afternoon.
Throughout, a part of his mind was on Jessica. To his
disappointment, she did not try and contact him
again. He was left to conclude that whatever she'd
wanted to tell him hadn't been important, or at least
not of a life-and-death nature. And yet he couldn't
help but feel troubled and concerned. By seven o'clock
that evening, he knew what he had to do. He also
knew that he was bending the rules, and that despite
his inner reservations about his proposed actions, it
couldn't be helped.

LYNN WAS SO ANGRY she couldn't see straight. Knowing the only way to vent her emotions was to confront their source, she lashed out at Jack the second he opened his front door, not even bothering to say hello. "Why didn't you tell me Jessica called you at your office this afternoon?" It hurt, knowing he trusted the people Jessica had run away from a lot more than he trusted her. "You know how long I've been working on her case! The least you could've done was notify me." Instead, he'd acted as if she didn't even exist, as if everything they had shared over the weekend had been a lie.

Jack's face had been cautious when he first saw her. Now he was downright angry. Reaching out, he grabbed her arm and pulled her inside. The door shut behind her. Still not speaking, he released his grip on her arm and stalked into his living room, leaving her to follow.

He turned to face her. His lips had thinned into a white line. His eyes were hard and merciless. "If you'll calm down—" he began.

"The way I'm feeling right now I may never calm down!" She paced back and forth like a caged animal and shot him a look that let him know how betrayed she felt, how close she was to losing her temper completely.

He inhaled slowly. When he spoke his words were carefully enunciated and as sharp-edged as cut glass. "The only reason I told the Montgomerys about their daughter's call was because I knew how worried they are and because she expressly told my secretary her call to me was not of a doctor-patient nature."

Lynn knew all that; the Montgomerys had said as much. "Just how much did you mean to her anyway?" she asked, the angry words tumbling out of her mouth before she could stop them. "Was she in love with you? Is that what this is all about?" Was that why Jessica had left? Why she clung to Jack still?

"Lynn!" His voice was rough with aggravation. He was affronted she would even think such a thing.

But Lynn wasn't about to be shamed into withholding her questions, every one of which she felt was very valid. "I mean it, Jack. What's going on? Why would she call you and not her parents?" And why hadn't Jack called her? She felt unspeakably betrayed. She had trusted him and thought he trusted her. Apparently that was not so, and the realization was almost more than she could bear. She'd been letting Jack begin to mean too much to her.

Jack sent her a contemptuous look. "I don't know why she called me. Maybe because I was the only one here she could trust."

Lynn was silent, realizing that was true. Jack wouldn't divulge Jessica's secrets, no matter how much pressure he was under from Lynn or Jessica's parents. Calming slightly, she decided to try another tack. "Do you know where she was calling from?"

"No," he said curtly, resenting her even asking.

Seeing he wasn't about to tell her anything more, Lynn became even more determined to find out. If he thought for one second she was just going to drop this, he was mistaken. It was her job and she would complete her mission with or without his help. Keeping her tone impeccably polite, her eyes never leaving the hard, angry lines of his face, she asked, "Will you let me trace—"

"No, Lynn." His tone was flat, final, obliterating the hope in hers. "I did that once. Looking back on it, I think I was wrong. Professionally, I've overstepped my bounds on this case."

"I don't see how." Lynn fumed.

"Jessica's an adult. She's free to come and go. You and I may not like that. Her parents may not like that. But we have no right to interfere, either individually or in a group."

"What if she needs help?" She resented his mocking tone and supercilious manner.

"Then I have to trust her to ask for it. She's already called twice," he reminded her hotly when she would have protested his decision. "I have every reason to believe she'll call again."

"And in the meantime?" Lynn's rage was icy and potent, as was the look in her eyes.

"We just wait." Face set, he watched her as if waiting for an emotional explosion. It didn't take long for him to get what he expected.

"Her parents are worried sick!" Lynn flung up her hands in agitation.

"They're also overpossessive," Jack argued, calmly sliding his hands into his pockets. His eyes narrowed. "Why do you think Jessica's been running so hard and so long?" Without warning, his voice softened,

"Look, I know you care about what happens to her and want to protect her."

"You're damn right I do. It's my job!"

"But you're going to have to put that aside and just back off."

"What if I don't want to back off?" She started toward him, meeting him halfway in the middle of the room. Her chin was up, and her hands were planted defiantly on her waist.

Then it was all over between them, she saw it by the look on his face. But that wasn't what she wanted. She needed his help on this case. In her personal life, she needed his support. She might not like it, but those were the facts.

Lynn sighed, turning away from him. She rubbed her neck, but the massaging motions did little to dissipate the tension she was feeling. The silence continued. Finally she turned back to Jack, saw that he was waiting for her to come to her senses. How was it possible he knew so much, saw so much? About her, about people in general? Was it the fact that he was a psychiatrist and studying people was his business? She supposed it didn't matter, it was enough he knew what was going on with her and with everyone else in this traumatic mess. "You really understand Jessica, don't you?" she said softly, envying his knowledge of the quarry she was chasing.

He shrugged, for once willing to talk about his ex-patient. "It's no secret she hasn't lived up to her parents' expectations. I know how rough that can be on a kid her age." He moved toward Lynn, partially closing the distance between them.

Lynn swallowed hard, fighting the knot of emotion welling up in her throat. She was tired and frustrated. She wanted this tension between them to end. She wanted to understand him better, too.

Jack took yet another step closer. Hand on her spine, he led her gently to the sofa and sat down beside her. "You see, although I get along with my folks now it wasn't always so. I was the only child, the only son, and as such, I was encouraged and expected to follow in my father's footsteps."

"But you became a doctor instead."

"Yeah."

"Your father disapproved of that?"

Jack made a seesawing motion with his right hand, and then elaborated sadly, "He never said anything, but when I looked in his eyes I always knew how he felt. Later he took on a partner—a protégé—a bright ambitious kid just out of law school. That seemed finally to satisfy his need to pass down both his wisdom and the practice he'd built. But for a while there, it was rough going and many times I wished I could just get the hell out of there, run away and never come back. Anything so I wouldn't have to see that disappointed look in my dad's eyes."

"And you think that's all it is with Jessica?" Vaguely, she was aware that he had captured her hand, and that the warmth of his fingers covering hers felt very good.

Jack was silent, and for a moment she thought he wouldn't answer. He might be considering that if he did he'd be revealing too much about what he knew of Jessica from her sessions with him. "I don't know," he said finally. "I just know that for me the borders of right and wrong have begun to blur here and I don't want that. I can't live that way. I don't think you should ask me to live that way, either."

She saw his point. But her need to solve this puzzle was also very strong. She knew she wouldn't be able to live with herself if something happened to Jessica before they found her, not if Lynn could have done something to help. And she was worried about Jessica, after this second phone call. She looked at Jack, wanting his promise, wanting to know he wasn't turning his back on this young woman. Or Lynn. Or the Montgomerys. "But if Jessica needs help—"

"Andrea confirmed she didn't threaten suicide."

"Maybe so, but she's not happy." Lynn was irritated Jack wasn't more concerned, that he was withdrawing his help and full cooperation.

Jack released his grip on her hand. "Many people aren't happy. That's no reason to invade their privacy."

Lynn tried not to notice how bereft her hand felt. Or how hurt she was when he got up from the sofa and walked away. "You really won't help me trace the phone call to your office?" She couldn't believe he would actually say no to her.

"No, I won't."

Maybe if she just gave him time to cool off, Lynn thought. "Does she know I'm looking for her?" Lynn asked, struggling to put aside her hurt and take this new difficulty in stride, much as she would've with any other letdown. "Do you think she's seen the ads in the paper?"

"She didn't say anything, and I don't think she knows about the ads. But I think she may well have anticipated something like this happening. She's a bright young woman. She knows her parents pretty well."

"If I just knew what city the call was made from—"

"Lynn, forget it!"

Lynn stared at him in growing fury and frustration. She hated his hot-and-cold attitude, one minute willing to help her, the next not. "Don't you want her to come home?"

Jack's expression remained stony. "Only if it's what she wants and that's for her to decide." With studied insolence, he sank into a chair and stretched his long legs out in front of him, so they were seated on opposite sides of the room. "She's a grown woman, Lynn, even if her parents—and you—don't want to admit that."

Lynn swore beneath her breath, making no effort to hide her irritation as they studied each other relentlessly, like two boxers about to step into the ring. It was clear to her the question-and-answer session—as unproductive as it had been—was over. She knew she'd pressed him as far as she could. She wasn't happy he'd cut her out, but given the circumstances she understood very well why he had. The only thing she could do now was try to alter the way he behaved in the future. Taking a deep breath, she made her tone sensible and sweet, "Jack, if she calls again—"

"If given the opportunity, I'll relay the fact her folks are worried about her and would like to hear from her, that's all."

He wasn't being much help, she thought, her temper rising again. With effort, Lynn kept her tone level. "You won't tell her I'm looking for her?" If Jessica knew for a fact she had a detective on her trail, there was no telling what she'd do. Lynn didn't want her running now if she could prevent it. More than likely her money was running out, and since she was unwilling to use her credit cards—no charges had been made on them since she ran away—she'd have to look for a job soon and settle down somewhere. Which meant leaving a trail. And once she did, Lynn would be able to find her, she was sure of it. Whether Jack helped or not!

"I don't want to upset her, so no, I won't tell her you're looking for her. Not unless..." He paused uncertainly.

A shudder of despair went down Lynn's spine; she and Jack were never going to see eye to eye on this. "Unless what?" she demanded a trifle impatiently.

Jack stopped slouching and sat up ramrod straight in his chair. His jaw became iron hard. "Unless it's somehow relevant to the conversation. My first concern here, Lynn, my first commitment has to be my patient.''

His condescending attitude was annoying. "My first obligation is to my client,'' she responded, and she wasn't going to let him get in the way of that.

"Fine. Now do you mind if we just drop this?'' His eyes turned a stormier color of blue and he raked both hands through his hair. "We're never going to agree on this.''

She stared at him unhappily. It wasn't so much his refusal to help her as the lack of respect she saw on his face. He thought she was in the wrong for being so diligent, so absorbed in her work. And that she couldn't stand. It reminded her too much of her ex-husband.

"You're disappointed in me, aren't you?'' he asked unhappily, realizing she was equally at a loss.

Lynn nodded. "I expected more.''

"I could say the same thing.''

Wetting her lips, she tried once more to reason with him. "Rules are—''

"Meant to broken?'' Again, his low voice was underscored with contempt.

"Maybe,'' Lynn allowed defiantly, hating his low censuring tone.

He shook his head and said curtly, "I disagree.''

Suddenly, she realized they'd said everything that had to be said, and were no closer to working out a solution than they had been when she arrived. "Let me know if you change your mind,'' she said quietly, starting for the door.

"You're leaving?" He followed her, his feelings as mixed as hers. She saw he didn't want her to go, but she knew—from her experience living with Robert after her investigation of him—that it did no good for two people to spend time with each other when they were at such odds over the way they lived their lives and pursued their own ideals. To do so now with Jack would only accentuate and aggravate their differences, and that she didn't think she could stand. It hurt enough as it was.

She nodded slowly. "I think it's best." She didn't want to fight with him. And she knew if they talked until dawn they would never agree. As long as he kept his contemptuous attitude about what she did for a living, about her commitment to her work, nothing was possible between them.

NOLAND CAME HOME from the hospital on Friday. Gail was there to help him settle in. While, she was in the kitchen helping Sid prepare some tea, Lynn remained behind to keep her brother company. The one ray of sunshine in her life was her brother's renewed closeness with his estranged wife. "Things are looking good for you and Gail, huh?"

A look of pain crossed Noland's face. "Look, I know how much you like Gail, but don't read too much into this, okay, sis? She feels a little guilty, that's all. That's the only reason she's here."

"Guilty?" Lynn repeated, shocked. "For what?"

"For divorcing me when she still loves me, and she knows I love her."

"Noland, you can't be serious. Surely you two can't be thinking of continuing with this lunacy! After all the time she's spent with you at the hospital the past week? She doesn't want this divorce, Noland. If she hasn't said so directly, it's because she probably didn't want to overwhelm you."

Noland looked away, then changed the subject, refusing to talk further about his impending divorce. "So where's Jack been lately?" he said genially. "Dad says he hasn't been around the past two days."

Lynn didn't want to talk about that. "We've both been busy," she lied.

Noland raised his brows. "Not that busy. He dropped by my hospital room twice to say hello."

Jack's concern for her brother heartened Lynn. That meant he hadn't completely cut himself off from her family, even if he hadn't tried to talk to her again. Apparently he had decided, as she did, that some distance was necessary between them for now if they were ever to work everything out. "Oh."

Noland gave her a hard look. "What's going on between the two of you?"

Briefly Lynn explained. Noland was quiet a long moment. He'd never been big on rules himself, so he understood Lynn's point of view. He also understood Jack's. "I don't know, sis. I think you're in a very sticky situation."

"Tell me about it," she lamented.

"Are you still mad at Jack for not letting you trace that call into his office?"

"Yes. And no." Lynn paused. "The truth is I don't want Jack to do anything that makes him uncomfortable. I just wish this had never come up between us. That we could've met and had a romance or a friendship or whatever without this extraneous stuff going on."

"Did you tell him that?" Noland asked sympathetically.

"No." Lynn straightened the several pots of flowers sent by well-wishers to brighten up his hospital room.

"Why not?" Her brother looked at her steadily.

"Well, he hasn't called."

"Since when did you forget how to use the phone?"

Lynn blushed. Leave it to her brother to get right to the point. "I don't want to make a nuisance of myself."

"Better to do that than lose out on something altogether," he said glumly.

"Are we talking about your situation now or mine?" she asked gently, wishing for the thousandth time that he and Gail wouldn't divorce.

"Yours. Mine is over."

"Noland—"

"Call him, Lynn, don't wait too long to do it. You're the one who's always going for broke to get what you want, and if I know my sister, you want Jack more than anything else."

Chapter Eleven

Lynn did make a call, but it was to Walter to arrange a meeting. She had the answers to his case and although she knew they would hurt him, she decided it was best that he be told as soon as possible. At the appointed hour, she showed up at his house and was very shocked to find Jack there also. She should have known that Walter would have mentioned the meeting to him, and of course he, with his protective instincts in full force, would have made a point of being there.

Steeling herself to disclose her discoveries and get out of there as soon as possible—and be finished not just with the case but with Jack as well—she began. "I've got some bad news. You know that land you've got your eye on? It's already been sold."

"To whom?" Walter demanded, both indignant and surprised.

"The Cumberland Corporation."

"Know anything about them?"

Lynn met his gaze straight on, trying not to let her eyes stray toward Jack. "It's a holding company. Land prices in the area are already going up substantially."

"As they get ready for us to try to buy."

"Right."

"Any idea who's behind it?"

Lynn swallowed hard. "So far I've only uncovered a couple of names." She took a deep breath, knowing there was no easy way to tell him. "Well, to put it bluntly, one of them is—"

"It's Sheila, isn't it?" he asked. His face held a resigned expression.

"How did you guess?" Lynn was astounded.

Walter sighed. "Her husband wasn't the most scrupulous in his dealings. As a matter of fact, he was a scoundrel. I hoped . . . she looked so innocent. . . ." His fingers clenched into fists. "A fool, that's what I am. Maybe you're right, Jack—maybe I am losing the ability to judge. Maybe I just see what I want to see anymore."

Jack touched his uncle's shoulder compassionately. "Look, this could have happened to anyone. So you believe in people and aren't afraid to trust them. There's nothing wrong with that." He and Lynn exchanged glances. "In fact, in today's world, that's admirable."

"Mr. Ohlendorf, even I didn't suspect!" Lynn exclaimed, also wanting to allay his feelings of self-reproach.

"Nor did I," Jack said emphatically. "And we're both trained observers." Suddenly Lynn felt as if she and Jack were a team again and no longer enemies.

Walter was silent, and Jack prepared to leave, motioning to her to do the same. She realized that it would be best if Walter were left to himself for now. There wasn't anything anybody could do or say at this point to make him feel better. But she didn't worry about him. Walter had such a zest for living that she was sure he would soon recover from this setback and go on.

"Thanks for uncovering this," Jack said in a soft voice as soon as they were out the front door.

She flushed at his sincere gratitude. It felt good, knowing he respected her again, that he thought she'd not only done a good job but provided a valuable service as well. "I was glad to help," Lynn said calmly. "Although I'm not happy about the results."

He led her to the porch swing. "I've missed you," he said simply as soon as they'd sat down. "More than I bargained on."

Lynn had missed him, too. She felt her eyes water and her throat close. All she could think of was how much she wanted to feel his mouth on hers and have his arms around her once again.

He seemed to realize all she felt and all she feared. He covered her hands with his own. His grip was warm, strong and very sure. "So to that end, I have a proposal," he said in an affectionate tone, not giving her a chance to talk about Jessica. "I want us to forget everything else that's been going on, driving us apart, and start over.''

Days ago Lynn wasn't sure she could do that. Now she didn't know how she could not. "Put everything else on the back burner?" she asked, wanting to make sure she knew what he meant.

He cared enough about her to be honest. "I still don't want to be directly involved on the Montgomery case, not anymore.''

Lynn wished he would be involved, but she'd also had time to think since they quarreled. She understood where he was coming from and respected his need to distance himself from her investigation. "What did you have in mind?" she asked, realizing her pulse had speeded up, in pleasure and anticipation.

He tightened his grip on her hands, looking very much as if he wanted to kiss her then and there. "That we pick up where we left off, before the fight.''

"Nothing's changed," she said softly, wanting to reconcile, but not wanting to push all the problems aside—knowing they'd be bound to surface again later on. "I'm still on that case." The case that had driven them apart.

His eyes darkened, but the affection in his eyes didn't lessen. With difficulty, and looking both vulnerable and tired, he confessed, "I know that. I know we still have our differences. It's not my wish to pass judgment on anyone. And I'm sorry if it seemed I was excluding you from that last phone call. I never meant to hurt you.''

She believed him, but he had been contemptuous and disapproving of her, and those were two attitudes she didn't want in any man she was with. They made for too much hurt and anger.

Jack felt strongly their differences could be overcome, if only she understood him. "It's just that I was beginning to feel as if my life was totally dominated by problems and complications—your cases and my ex-patients. I can't function in a work-dominated environment, Lynn." His eyes met hers earnestly, and his mouth softened just a bit. "I need some breathing space, some time alone. And not just for myself, but for us," he finished, his hand lightly tracing patterns on hers. He waited until he saw her start to smile. "So, what do you say? Would you like to try it again?"

"Try what?" Lynn teased, unaccountably feeling ridiculously happy. "Dating?" She had hoped this would happen all along, that they would find a way to get past their differences. Just as it had apparently happened for Gail and Noland, although the two were still too stubborn to admit what they were feeling.

Jack shrugged, his expression relieved as he leaned closer to her. His low voice was underscored with the same happiness she felt. "We could spend a night on the town. Just the two of us alone. No problems, no complications, no work."

"Just you and me." Lynn savored the idea. Her smile deepened. She sighed. "Sounds good. Sounds great."

THEY HAD THAT NIGHT out alone and several more. It was as if they'd never been apart, and yet their relationship became deeper, more special, because of the few but heartbreaking days they'd spent apart. They cherished each other more and didn't take each other for granted. And they didn't allow their work to dominate the time they spent together.

They had their whimsical moments. Returning home from a Kenny Loggins concert, Lynn was thinking about the groups of teenagers that had attended. They all looked so happy, so carefree. Although she didn't want to go back to the uncertainty of her youth, the trauma of growing up, sometimes she wished she were still so carefree. "Why so pensive?" Jack asked as he pulled up and parked in front of her house.

Lynn snuggled deeper into her wool coat. They'd had their first frost the night before; it looked as if they were in for the second. "Oh, I was just thinking I wish we'd known each other sooner. When we were kids. I think I would've liked to date you in high school."

Jack helped her out, wrapped his arms around her waist and drew her close to his side. "You think so, hmm?" he teased.

They walked toward her front door. The lights were on inside. Jack had already decided he wouldn't stay since they both had to work the next day. But she was in no hurry to get inside. "Mmm-hmm." A cold breeze swept through the trees, and she moved closer to his side. She laced her arm through his. "You were probably a jock, popular, the kind of guy girls go wild over.''

''And what were you like? A tomboy?''

''Yep. One hundred per cent.'' Lynn leaned against the front door.

One arm stretched above her head, he smiled down at her. ''I bet you had a lot of dates, too.''

Lynn was so aware of him she could barely breathe. ''I did and I didn't. I couldn't find anybody to get serious about.'' The collar of his jacket was turned in. She reached up and straightened it.

''And you wanted to—get serious about someone.'' He moved closer until his warm breath caressed her temple.

''Oh, yes.'' She'd wanted to be married and settled down for as long as she could remember. Only it had never seemed to work out that way. His face and hair seemed gilded by moonlight. She was glad her father had tactfully left the front porch light off. She much preferred saying her good-nights against a starry sky.

''Too bad it's impossible to turn back the clock.'' Caught staring at her mouth, he dragged his eyes back to hers.

Lynn smiled. ''I know. I would've gotten a kick out of seeing you as you were then.''

His eyes glimmered with a sudden idea. His smile deepened mysteriously. ''You know, there's no reason why you couldn't see me now as I was then. Or vice versa.''

"What do you mean? Pictures?" She still had her old yearbooks and she wouldn't mind seeing his. His eyes were like magnets, drawing her.

"I'll go you one better. We'll have a come-as-you-were-date, circa your senior year in high school."

"You're serious?" A familiar warmth settled into her middle.

"Absolutely. You game?"

Lynn grinned, loving the affection she saw on his face. "Why not?" she said dryly. "I've always loved adventure."

"WELL, THAT'S A NEW ONE," Noland said Saturday night as Lynn came down the stairs. "I haven't seen you in a miniskirt and white boots since—"

"Never mind when that was," Lynn cut her brother off and moved to the mirror to primp. She felt a little bare. She hadn't worn a miniskirt for years. Thank goodness she still had the figure for it; thank goodness shorter skirts were coming back in style.

The doorbell rang. "I'll get it!" Lynn rushed to the door.

She couldn't open it soon enough. From the other side of the portal, Jack stared at her, entranced, taking in her hair, which had been put up on hot rollers and styled in wild gypsy curls, the subtle makeup she wore on her face and the birthstone necklace around her neck. Stepping inside, his gaze drifted lower. He smiled approvingly at her outfit, then nodded and looked some more at the girlish blue-paid wool miniskirt, white blouse and matching blue knit vest. Her class ring was on her finger.

"Hi," he drawled softly, grinning from ear to ear and looking as if he was ready for adventure. "You look great!"

"Thanks," Lynn said shyly. He was standing very close. His sheer physicality overwhelmed her—she knew what it felt like to be held in his arms, against the solid wall of his chest, with his thighs brushing hers. "So do you. In fact, you're just as I imagined you would be." He was wearing a gray and blue letter jacket, very worn jeans, a football jersey emblazoned with his name and the number fifty-one, and worn black and white high-top sneakers. He wore a senior key around his neck and his class ring on his finger.

Noland sauntered into the front hall as Lynn gathered up the navy midicoat she'd found in the attic, along with the long scarf, hat, and mittens. He shook his head in exaggerated disbelief. "I hate to tell you guys this," he said, "but Halloween was over last week."

"Was it?" Lynn pretended to look surprised, confused and dismayed all at once.

Jack only smiled mysteriously.

Noland looked them both up and down. "I don't suppose you're going to let me in on what you're doing?"

"Nope." Lynn smiled firmly.

Her father walked into the hall. He took one look at Lynn and Jack and shook his head in amusement. Not commenting on either of their appearances, he said, "Have fun, you two. Mind your own business, Noland."

Giggling, and without enlightening Noland, they went out the door and down the drive to Jack's car. Startled, Lynn stopped some six feet away from the vehicle—a battered red and black sports car with a patched convertible top instead of his late-model BMW. "Where'd you get this?"

"I borrowed it from a friend. It's something, isn't it?"

He could say that again. "You really are going all out, aren't you?" she asked wryly.

"You wanted to know what I was like then. A heap like this was all I could afford to drive."

She shook her head in reluctant admiration. "Yet you went for status, too—a sports car."

With a terrible stick shift and a motor that made a racket, it turned out. Lynn huddled in the front seat as the cool night air wafted around them. Jack definitely had the spirit of adventure, she decided. "Where are we going?" She tried to keep her teeth from chattering.

"To a double feature. James Bond. It's at one of those bargain rate theaters near the university. You know the kind with little heat, lousy refreshments and terrible seats?"

She groaned, both at his description of the theater in which they were going to spend the next four-plus hours and his selection of films. "Don't tell me," she said dryly, "007 was one of your favorite heroes when you were a kid."

Jack nodded seriously. "I wanted to be just like him. Women, danger, excitement. That man had it all!"

Usually it was all Lynn could do to sit through one Bond movie. However, she supposed it could have been worse. He could have been a nut about horror flicks in his teens. "Which 007 is it? Roger Moore or Sean Connery?"

"Connery in both."

"Oh, well."

He slanted her an inquiring glance.

She blushed. "Okay, you've got me," she confessed, feeling a blush heat her face at his knowing glance. "I think Sean Connery's terribly sexy." She practically drooled just watching him on the big screen.

Jack's grin widened. He shook his head with amused disdain. "Women! And you accuse us guys of being salacious!"

Lynn had to admit Jack picked a good place for their date. Even dressed as they were, they drew few glances from the eclectically dressed college crowd. Jack loaded up on a huge tub of buttered popcorn, two packs of candy and two Cokes. As they made their way to their seats, Lynn carrying the Cokes, Jack tripped unexpectedly. He caught himself before he fell, but just barely. Popcorn littered the aisle. There were echoes of laughter around them, including a few chuckles from Jack and Lynn themselves.

There was also a boyish gleam in Jack's eyes. "Did you do that on purpose?" she whispered after they sat down.

"Who, *moi*? Lynn, how could you even accuse me of such a thing?"

Because the way to a woman's heart, she thought, was to make her laugh. And all teenage guys knew that!

"When I was seventeen a lack of coordination came naturally," Jack confided, leaning over to whisper in her ear. He took her hand in his. "This, too," he whispered as the movie started, "is de rigueur."

Lynn found she enjoyed the hand-holding, the popcorn, even the two Bond movies.

Afterward Jack took her to a drive-in hamburger stand. They ordered cheeseburgers, fries and onion rings and cherry colas. While they ate, teenagers socialized through open car windows and drove round and round the lighted portico. "This takes me back," Lynn said smiling and demurely crossing her legs at the knee as she watched a couple flirting across the way. The small sports car left little in the way of leg room. Her knees were practically up to her chin, her skirt was up her thigh, no matter how much she tugged and pulled in her efforts to regain a little modesty.

"Me, too," Jack said softly. "Did you do a lot of dating when you were growing up?"

"Yeah, I did." She noticed his glance straying up her legs, and back down.

"Run around with your girlfriends a lot?" he asked, his voice dropping another notch.

"That, too." His husky voice was doing strange things to her middle again. She shifted restlessly in her seat.

Jack, however, seemed caught up in uncovering as much as possible about her past. "I bet you had a nickname, too." Lynn nodded, and he said, "Let me see if I can guess it. Legs?"

Lynn grinned. He could act as innocent as he wanted, but he did have a one-track mind. "Nope."

"Hmm." Jack frowned. "That surprises me." He slanted another look at her limbs. "You do have terrific legs, you know. And they're especially attractive in that short skirt." He grinned.

Lynn resisted the urge to tug the hem down. "I think this is the part where I bash you with my purse," she said. "At the very least, sock you in the arm."

"No rude comments from the guys, huh?"

"Not a one."

"Okay." He made a great show of straightening up. "Back to the guessing game." He squinted at her, scowled as if deep in thought. "How about Blondie?" he said finally.

"Wrong again." She laughed softly, enjoying the game—and his company.

"Surely you weren't a Buffy or a Bunny!"

"No, thank God."

He shrugged. "I've run out of guesses."

"They called me Rescuer because I was always coming to someone's aid."

Jack's glance darkened but he made no move to touch her. "Early signs of your becoming a cop, huh?"

"I guess. What about you? What was your nickname?" she asked curiously.

"They used to call me Bones because I was so skinny. I ate constantly but just couldn't seem to gain any weight."

"Well, you've filled out perfectly now."

He grinned, taking the compliment well. "In that case—" his eyes glittered teasingly "—wanna go park?"

"Jack!"

He slid toward her, as much as the stick shift would allow, and cupped an audacious hand over her knee. "I'm seventeen, remember?" he reminded in his best bad-boy tone. "All hormones and emotions? With a one-track mind?"

Hopeful, too. "Yeah, well, I'm seventeen, too, tonight." She tactfully removed his hand from her knee and dropped it back into his lap. "And my dad has a midnight curfew for me so I won't be led off the primrose path by guys with one-track minds."

He snapped his fingers regretfully. "Darn. And I thought I did everything just right tonight. Impressing you with my car, tripping at just the right moment to make you and everyone else giggle!"

"So you did do that on purpose!"

"You knew I did."

"Yeah."

He looked suddenly as if he wanted very much to kiss her and didn't know if he would be able to stop once he started. "Midnight, curfew hmm?" he asked softly.

Lynn nodded. Going home really wasn't what she wanted, but she also knew it would be wise. The way she was feeling tonight it would be all too easy to give herself to Jack. She already knew he cared about her. She saw it in his eyes every time he looked at her. But there was still so much she had to learn about him, and he her. Maybe it was old-fashioned, but she wanted to be sure first before she went to bed with him that theirs was a romance that would last. She didn't want either of them regretting any of their actions later.

"Saved by the rules," Jack said softly.

Lynn nodded, knowing the save wasn't going to be for very long, not if Jack's intense look was any indication. She'd thought earlier they were destined to be together. Now she knew it was so.

"IF I'D KNOWN you were going to work me this hard, I'm not sure I would've come over!" Lynn teased indignantly, seven and a half dates later. It seemed forever since she and Jack had reconciled their differences and begun seeing each other again. But then, it seemed not nearly long enough. He'd helped her laugh again and forget everything but the moment and the magic they were both feeling. He helped her find the beauty in every moment, large or small, and for that she would be forever grateful.

Walter, too, had recovered from his disappointment. He was still interested in a resort for senior citizens, but this time he intended to buy the land himself and then approach other investors. Sheila and her cohorts had been exposed, and she had fled town even before the story appeared in the papers. Wherever she was, Lynn hoped she wasn't getting her claws on some poor unsuspecting widows.

The Montgomery case, on the other hand, had not had any new developments. Contrary to Lynn's high hopes, the photo ads had netted plenty of prank calls and letters but no single lead. There really was nothing to be done now but to wait and hope. In the meantime, she was determined not to let the frustration of being stymied at work interfere with her happiness with Jack.

He waved a gloved index finger in her face. "Hey, I promised to rake *your* leaves tomorrow."

"Yeah, I know." And it was a good thing, too. Neither her brother nor her father were up to it physically—Noland because he was still recovering from his surgery, and her dad because his bursitis had been acting up again. But had Lynn not insisted on doing it, one or the other would have been out hauling leaves.

He pulled her to him. "Come on, tell the truth, you don't really mind, do you?"

Their cheeks and noses were pink with the cold. Their breath puffed out white and smoky every time they laughed or spoke.

"Well..." She grinned at Jack, just happy to be with him.

"Besides, yard work is so much more fun when it's done together." He pressed a light kiss on her lips. Her stomach rose and fell as weightlessly as a balloon. He smiled and lowered his voice a devastating notch. "Want to go inside and get some cider?"

As always, when he touched her, she felt herself grow soft and warm and pliant. Reluctantly Lynn cast a backward glance at the scattered leaves. Yes, she wanted to go inside. To cuddle and kiss. Never had she met a man who liked to kiss as much as Jack. And who was as good at it, making it a satisfying love act in itself.

Their decision made, they wasted no time getting inside, shedding coats and mittens. "You get the cinnamon sticks. I'll heat the water for the cider," Jack said, pointing Lynn toward the pantry.

It took Lynn several minutes to find what she needed; it seemed Jack packed everything in unlabeled airtight containers. By the time she'd emerged with the cinnamon, Jack was pouring hot water into the cups and adding instant mix. She stood beside him, watching as steam rose from the cups.

The heavy aroma of apples and spice filled the kitchen. He handed her a cup, and they sipped gingerly, being careful not to burn their mouths. "Mmm, this is good," Lynn said, savoring the sweetness.

"Better than hot chocolate?"

"Definitely."

She took another sip and put her cup down. So did Jack.

The moment drew out.

They'd gone into his house, looking for a respite from work. But suddenly that wasn't what Lynn wanted at all. Nor did Jack.

His hand found hers, squeezing it gently, then tracing delicate patterns on the sensitive inside of her wrist. She felt a shiver of anticipation run through her. She knew what he was asking. And she knew she wanted him, too. "Lynn," he said softly, "oh, Lynn."

"I like the way you say my name," she whispered. Lifting his hand to her mouth, she pressed a kiss into his palm. He groaned.

"And I like the way you look. I like the way you smell and feel and talk and act—"

"And kiss?" she asked playfully, tilting her head back to his.

"That, too." His throat was so hoarse he could barely get the words out. And then the time for talking, for flirting, was over.

Wordlessly he drew her to him, an arm hooked about her waist. As his mouth lowered to hers, a feeling of contentment swept through her. She knew with sudden clarity that he was the one man for her and always would be. It was time they dealt with their feelings, let themselves be as vulnerable and needy as it was possible for two people to be.

His lips fused with hers in a gentle bonding, transmitting an incredible love and tenderness. She melted against him, her knees turning to mush beneath her, and his constraint—what had been left of it—fled. His mouth became ardent, demanding. Helpless to do otherwise, she responded to his desire, returning it tenfold, until her pulse thudded erratically and she swayed against him, barely able to stand. *Oh God,* she thought, *I never want this moment to end.*

His skin felt hot. And he touched her in a way that was just short of maddening, his fingers trailing lightly over her spine and down her hips, asking permission and hoping she would give it. And she realized with a fast growing impatience that she wanted more, that she wanted all of him, and that she wanted to show him how grateful she was that he had dispelled the loneliness from her life.

He deepened the kiss, his tongue plunging into the willing sweetness of her mouth. His hips moved against hers, hard, demanding. "Oh God, Lynn." Shudders wracked him. His breathing came fast, his forehead was beaded with sweat.

She felt the hardness of his arousal through the thin wool of her pants, and the cessation of his kiss was like a sharp pain. "Don't stop," she whispered, feeling inexplicably bereft and needing his kisses to feel whole, his warmth to feel loved.

He groaned against her skin, his mouth following the long slender line of her throat. She arched into him, until their taut, trembling bodies complemented each other's perfectly. When he slid his fingers over the front of her shirt, she sucked in her breath and found herself moving to allow him the room he needed. Frissons of sensation swept through her, like ribbons of fire. Slowly he unbuttoned her blouse and released the front catch on her bra. His gaze lingered hotly on her pale creamy skin crowned with the color and texture of deep rose silk.... He suckled her breasts, unleashing curling waves of heat throughout her.

Only when the buds were as swollen and well-kissed as her mouth did he cease his tender ministrations. He straightened slowly and she reeled from the depth of need she saw in his eyes and the depth of pleasure she had already given him.

He led her to his bedroom. "You're beautiful. Perfect," he whispered, drawing her down onto the sheets. His hands moved lovingly over her skin, tracing every hollow, every curve. She had never felt so revered. Her heart thudding, she, too, explored his body. They gazed into each other's eyes, entranced, caught up in the spell of what was happening.

He moved into her, and she was gasping, awash with sensation, throbbing with need. He moved to an erotic rhythm until Lynn was clutching him to her greedily, sure she could stand it no longer. Past the point of restraint, he moaned and then whispered her name and catapulted them both past the edge.

Long moments later, they drifted slowly back to reality. They remained locked in each other's arms. He was holding her as if he would never let her go. Lynn's contentment deepened.

She felt his cheek against her hair, then his lips moving gently across her temple. "I love you," he whispered, gathering her closer, holding her near.

"And I love you," Lynn whispered back.

She didn't want to think about the future. She didn't want to think about the complications. She just wanted to savor that moment, that man. She wanted to hold on to what they'd found, and keep holding on.

Chapter Twelve

The next few days were a dream come true for Lynn and Jack. They saw each other every night. They made love every night. They shared their hopes and dreams.

Unfortunately, her happiness was in direct contrast to Noland's melancholy mood. From talking to Gail Lynn knew she was blue, too. Unable to stand it any longer, she decided to do something about it. But she couldn't do it alone.

"I don't think interfering's a good idea, Lynn," Jack began sternly when she went to him with her idea that was guaranteed to bring her whole family happiness.

She had braced herself for resistance. She said softly, "Why not? You know how much Gail cares about him. And I know he's still desperately in love with her." Noland had told her so when he came home from the hospital, and she'd related that conversation to Jack.

"Lynn, the two of them are getting a divorce," Jack said wearily.

"I know," she said, anxiously biting her lip. "The final hearing is slated for next week. Oh, please, Jack, help me out on this. I just want them to be alone together for a few hours. That's all I'm asking. Just enough time for them to start to talk things out in a neutral setting that could also turn romantic." Somewhere they wouldn't be disturbed.

Jack studied her for several moments. It was hard to know what he was thinking. His initial disdain had faded under the force of her gentle persuasion. "You're really determined to do this, aren't you?"

She nodded slowly, admitting, "Whether you help me or not. Jack, I know they belong together. And Noland's been so miserable." He hadn't been eating or sleeping. She felt sick at heart just thinking about it.

"You know how I feel about meddling," he said impatiently.

"And you know how I feel about helping people."

Jack cocked a cynical eyebrow. "There's a difference between interfering and aiding." His caustic tone intimated she had yet to learn that difference.

Knowing he was right, that it was wrong to meddle in someone else's love life, Lynn blushed and raised both hands in an open admission of surrender. "Okay, okay, you're right. It is sneaky of me to be planning this." She leaned forward, both hands flat on the table in front of her. "But I am not going to stand idly by and just watch them end this marriage without trying to save it. I'd never forgive myself it I let that happen." She couldn't, not when she loved her brother as much as she did.

His expression turned thoughtful. "He'll be furious with you, as will Gail."

Lynn knew that, too. And she was prepared to weather any storm to get the happy ending they all deserved. "They'll get over it once they work things out. In fact, they'll probably be grateful. Oh, please, Jack, please. Just lend me the keys to your houseboat. You don't even have to do anything. I'll take care of everything. You won't even have to be involved."

There was another silence as he took in her determined expression. Without warning, the grim lines around his mouth relaxed. His eyes became brighter, his expression amused. She saw with relief she'd won him over. "All right," Jack said finally. "If that's what you want, I'll help make it a day no one will ever forget."

"THIS IS A GREAT IDEA, taking the houseboat out on the lake," Gail began early Saturday morning. The weather was crisp and cool, with clear blue skies. "How'd you get Jack to loan it to us?"

"He knew you needed the time off," Lynn lied.

Gail nodded and stretched. "It has been a stressful few weeks with Noland getting shot and the final divorce hearing coming up." Sadness crossed her face as she stared out at the water.

"How do you feel about Noland now?" Lynn asked gently, guiding the boat across the still waters of the lake. The atmosphere was so restful here, she knew her plan was going to work.

Gail shrugged. "The same. I'll always love him, but it will never work. I just can't handle the stress of being a cop's wife, and he doesn't want to quit. It's better this way, Lynn. It really is." She turned to face Lynn, her expression serious.

"I don't see how you can say that," Lynn countered softly. It was criminal what these two were doing to one another.

"Yeah, well, walk a mile or two in my shoes, and see how you feel," Gail said. "I know, I know. To you danger is something that you face every day. But it's not that way for me." She leaned back in the passenger seat. "He's a friend—he'll always be that."

Lynn looked to the horizon. She cut the engine. "We'd better stop a minute. There's a speedboat coming up on us pretty fast."

Gail's brow creased. "I wonder what they want."

"I don't know. We'll have to see." Lynn pretended to be perplexed.

"Want me to put down the anchor?"

"Maybe you'd better," Lynn decided, being careful to keep her face expressionless. As soon as Gail had left the cabin, Lynn slipped the keys into her pocket and then strode out to follow Gail. Her excitement mounted as she realized it wouldn't be long now before Gail and Noland were forced to hash out their problems. Lynn knew this was going to work, that they'd thank her later.

Curious, Gail stepped to the railing. She paled slightly as she recognized the two men in the speedboat. "Noland and Jack. What are they doing here?" Gail turned to Lynn. "Did you know about this?" she demanded. "Was this Noland's idea?"

Lynn avoided what she couldn't answer truthfully, and concentrated instead on a minute specific. "I doubt Noland knew I'd be out here today. I didn't mention it to him or Dad. Now, now, don't overreact. Just stay cool," Lynn advised her sister-in-law calmly. She caught the rope Jack tossed her and tied the two boats together. The men boarded, Noland first, then Jack.

Lynn expected fireworks in the first degree. To her surprise, though, once face-to-face Noland and Gail couldn't seem to stop smiling at one another. Looking uncomfortable with the whole situation, Jack took Lynn's arm and led her into the cabin. "Let's give them a moment alone."

"All right," Lynn whispered back agreeably. She was pleased at the way Noland and Gail had greeted each other. They might not need to be stranded; they might elect to stay on the boat while Jack and Lynn took their preplanned spin in the speedboat.

Lynn glanced out the front windows of the boat. Gail and Noland were standing close together, their heads bent. They looked very close suddenly. Lynn smiled, unable to contain her excitement. "It's working, isn't it? My plan is working."

Jack made a low sound in his throat. Wrapping an arm about her waist, he turned her toward the back of the boat and the twin bunks that took up the rear of the small cabin. "You sound surprised," he murmured, his eyes lingering on her mouth for a sexy moment.

Lynn flushed. "Well, I am. I guess. I don't know. The way the two of them have been insisting on this divorce," she whispered harshly, "I just didn't think they'd have a friendly word to say to each other, that's all."

"Funny. From where I stood, I didn't think they'd ever stopped being friends. Not really."

There was something on Jack's face that Lynn didn't like or trust. Despite his easygoing manner, he was looking too judgmental. Suddenly, the cabin felt too small, too crowded. She wondered what was on his mind, but couldn't discern anything, except that he was very pleased about something, while simultaneously remaining a little miffed at her for meddling.

"You're in a weird mood," she observed slowly.

He shrugged diffidently. "Yeah, I guess I am."

The coolness of the day had added color into his face. His eyes glittered a deep blue. He didn't drop his gaze, but kept staring at her with a mixture of aggravation and desire.

Lynn shifted uncomfortably and her heart began to thud. His grip on her waist tightened slightly. From the deck, she could hear soft voices. As Noland and Gail moved around the side of the deck, out of sight, she relaxed.

She had to stop worrying so much. So Jack was still mad at her for wanting to interfere in her brother's life, and for persuading him to take part in setting up the matchmaking ploy. He would get over it. It wasn't as if she did this sort of thing every day.

"Look," she whispered, needing to make sure he wasn't mad at her. "I know how you feel about meddling in general—"

He pinned her with that judgmental stare for several seconds, then gave her a smile. "You think I'm wrong to disapprove." His tone was cool.

Lynn began to get huffy. "I think we both need to look at the end results."

"Maybe we do at that," he said mysteriously.

Outside, the voices drifted farther away. There was a soft thud, like the sound of the rope hitting the deck of the boat, and then there was the sound of the speed boat's motor starting up.

Realization hit her. "Oh, no," Lynn rushed forward. She dashed out onto the deck just in time to see the white speed boat motoring away. "Have fun, you two!" Gail shouted. She and Noland were both waving and laughing as if the joke was on Lynn.

"You tipped them off," Lynn accused Jack.

Jack braced his arms against his chest and faced her sternly. "I felt it only fair they had a right to know. They've been through enough, Lynn, the past couple weeks. They don't need to endure your matchmaking, too."

His know-it-all attitude was insufferable. She stalked toward the wheel, intending to drive them back to the docks.

She sighed her annoyance—the keys were not in the ignition. Remembering she'd put them in her pocket, she pulled them out. But before she could shove the key in the direction of the ignition, Jack's hand closed resolutely over her wrist. Two seconds later, the keys were in his hand.

"Give me those keys back."

"Aren't you the one who liked the idea of seeing a fighting couple stranded on a boat in the middle of the lake?" he asked sweetly.

She blew out an exasperated breath. "That was when it was Gail and Noland. And it was for their own good, Jack."

"Well, this, Lynn, is for your own good." He threw the keys high into the air and over the side of the boat. She watched, stunned and dismayed as they plopped into the deep, swirling gray-green waters and disappeared from sight.

"All right, Jack, the joke's over, and it was on me," she said drily. "Where is your spare set of keys?"

"Noland's got them. He'll bring them back to us in exactly four hours," Jack finished, consulting his watch.

"This isn't funny," she said icily.

His face became fierce. "I didn't think so, either. However, perhaps having experienced the enforced good intentions of others, you'll learn a lesson, too. You might as well relax," he tossed over his shoulder as he sauntered around the deck. "We're not going anywhere."

"Wrong," Lynn said defiantly, heading for the opposite side. "*You're* not going anywhere. I can swim." And she planned to do just that. He was dead wrong if he thought he was going to keep her on that boat. Keys or no keys, she was getting out of there. Now.

Jack watched as Lynn stripped off her jacket and shoes, her temper working full force. He was tempted to laugh and probably would have had the situation not been so potentially dangerous. Knowing brute force would be rejected and fought, he merely turned an indifferent shoulder as she began peeling off the sweater she wore over her shirt. "Don't be stupid, Lynn. The water's forty degrees."

The gruff pronouncement made, he turned and went into the cabin. Long moments later, Lynn followed. She had cooled down, but she still didn't like what he had done to her. He knew how she felt; he would have hated being manipulated, too.

However, she had gotten herself into this mess, he reasoned. And now that it was over, it was time they both calmed down and started behaving like rational adults.

Giving her little attention, but aware of her just the same, Jack began pouring hot cocoa mix into cups. Water was heating on the small cookstove. "Care for some hot chocolate?" he asked, his look cordial.

She gave him a withering glance, then turned and strode out of the cabin.

He heard her go up to the deck on the roof of the houseboat. *Smart,* he thought. She'd gone the one place he couldn't observe her, not without going up there, too.

Minutes later he followed her, carrying a cup of cocoa up the ladder. She was sitting, knees folded up to her chest, her arms clasped around her legs. He set the cup of cocoa beside her, went back down to get the second cup and joined her. Though he could see she was shivering beneath the denim jacket, sweater and jeans, she hadn't moved to take the cocoa he'd made her. "Your cocoa's getting cold."

"So?" she sighed as if very tired or slightly aggravated, he couldn't tell which.

"It'd warm you up."

"*You* warm me up."

"I know."

She turned at the innuendo in his voice, her eyes full of rage and a hint of something else. The beginnings of desire? he thought. She turned around to glare at the water.

He grinned and sipped his cocoa. He knew her rage was working itself out.

"Anger doesn't bother you, does it?" She asked, swiveling slightly, so she could see his face.

"No, not a bit." But this distance between them did.

Wearily, she rested her chin on her knees. "I didn't mean to hurt them," she murmured. "I just wanted Gail and Noland to be together again."

"I know." He pulled her into his arms. It was cold and windy up on the roof, but having Lynn right next to him offered some warmth. "I didn't want to hurt you, either."

"But you did want to prove a point." Her lower lip took on a delicious pout.

He ran a hand gently beneath her chin. "It seems to me both points were made. You'll do what you want to do, and so will I."

She shook her head. "Not a very good way to start a relationship, is it?" she said wryly.

"No, but a very common one." He shivered as a particularly bitter wind cut through his jacket. "Want to go down below?" The sun had disappeared behind some heavy gray clouds. The water was getting more choppy. Jack was beginning to wish he had those keys he had dramatically tossed overboard. "There's a small kerosene heater down there. Doesn't add a whole lot of warmth, but it does help."

Lynn nodded and unhesitatingly took the hand he offered.

By the time he got the heater going, it had begun to rain. Soft steady drops pelted the boat. As the rain continued the wind died down. Jack closed the cabin door, drew the curtains and lit two small lamps. Lynn opened the picnic basket she'd packed for Noland and Gail. Jack spied champagne, pâté, cheese, crackers, grapes and apples, small slivers of a rich walnut torte.

"In case they had something to celebrate," she explained, catching his avaricious glance. Now that they had made up, he looked very happy, and his mood was transmitting itself to her.

"Or got hungry," Jack continued. "Which I am."

She looked at him, ignoring the low, sexy pitch of his voice and the desire evident in his eyes. "Me, too," she said, aware her stomach had been growling for some time. The meal she'd prepared did look fabulous. "Want to feast?" she asked, already knowing what his answer would be.

"I thought you'd never ask."

While Jack opened the champagne, Lynn spread out a tablecloth on the small booth. They sat opposite each other, their legs touching. Slowly, the cabin heated up.

"So how long until we're rescued?" Lynn asked, taking a small bite of pâté.

Jack consulted his watch; his grin widened. She saw how much he was enjoying himself. Exasperation welled up within her.

"Three and a half hours, give or take a few minutes."

She groaned, feigning much more misery than she actually felt, cradling her head in her hands.

"You'll live," Jack said, not the least bit dispirited.

"I don't know about that," Lynn muttered.

"I do," he said softly, his tone causing her to lift her eyes to his. What she saw there made her heart start pounding. "To us," Jack said softly, clinking his glass against hers. And then softer yet, "May we never do this again."

Lynn sipped her champagne. She could feel the warmth in his gaze; it was a tangible presence, reaching out to give her comfort. "At least not unwillingly," she added.

"It is kind of cozy, isn't it?" He looked around him with satisfaction and wonder, as if the place were suddenly new to him again.

Lynn made a low affirmative sound and took another sip of champagne. "Now that the cabin is heating up," she answered. Ensconced in this warm and cozy cabin, she could scarcely remember why they'd even been fighting. She only knew she wanted to be in his arms.

"Forgive me?" His hand covered hers.

She felt the warmth and caring in his touch; it worked like magic to uncoil the fury and resentment that had knotted in her middle. "Doesn't look as if I have much choice," Lynn sighed.

Whenever she was around him, she got all soft and pliant. It wasn't anything he asked for, just the way she became. She didn't understand it. She wasn't sure she wanted to analyze it to death; she just wanted to enjoy this feeling that blossomed in her when she was in his presence. Because it had never happened with anyone else before, and she was sure it would never happen with anyone but Jack.

He stretched out his legs, nudging hers. They continued to eat ravenously. "Amazing, that anything this good—" Jack held up a cracker spread with pâté "—can be made out of liver."

"I know." Lynn reached for an apple and began to cut it up into sections. She shared half with Jack. "When I was a kid, I hated liver."

"Me, too." He poured them both more champagne.

"Did your mother make you eat it?"

"Once every other week or so. Finally, to get out of it, I pretended a biological intolerance of it. I'd itch and scratch and sneeze every time I even smelled it cooking."

Lynn grinned, imagining Jack in such boyish shenanigans. "Were you allergic to it?"

"No, but my mother could never be sure I wasn't. She didn't want to risk a full-blown allergic reaction to any food, so I got out of it."

"My mother used to try and disguise the liver. She used everything from steak sauce, catsup or mustard, to deep frying it in a breaded coating."

"Did it work?"

"Nope." Lynn shook her head vehemently. "It still had that funny aftertaste I always hated. One bite and I knew what I was eating." She made a face, remembering.

"What about Noland?"

"He and Dad both loved it."

"Why do you suppose the pâté is so good?"

"Number one, because I made it. Don't look at me like I'm crazy, it's really not that hard if you have a good recipe. And number two, because in this particular recipe anyway, I also put in spices, veal, pork, and ham, and plenty of cognac and cream."

"Ah, that explains it."

"I covered up the taste and then some."

"This really is good."

"Thanks."

"You like to cook?" His eyes were gentle on hers, and again she felt herself grow warm.

"When I get the chance," she admitted softly. Her eyes shining, she looked at him. "I like to experiment, just try lots of different things. To me it's like a science lab only the results are—usually, anyway—edible. Unfortunately it's a lot of hassle to cook for one. Noland and Dad both are meat-and-potatoes fellas. They don't like anything that's heavily spiced or out of the ordinary."

He let his smile broaden slightly. "You can come to my place and experiment to your heart's content. I even promise to eat it."

"You haven't seen anything yet."

"I trust you."

Lynn took a sip of champagne, feeling decidedly warmer under his direct gaze. The rain was still falling softly on the roof. She felt deliciously stranded with him. The atmosphere was intimate, warm and alluring. An unexpectedly romantic turn for an afternoon that had started out to be such a disaster.

"The champagne's first-rate, too."

"All bubbly."

"And tart and mellow all at once."

"Yeah."

"You like champagne?"

Lynn nodded. "I don't have it often, though. Always gives me a headache the next day."

"You need to drink more water with it. The headache comes from being dehydrated." He got up to get her a glass of water, then stood by while she drank the entire eight ounces.

"I'll remember that," Lynn said. Jack sat next to her and they cuddled together. "I remember when I had my first glass of champagne," she waxed on sentimentally. "I was sixteen."

"Your father permitted that?"

"Not exactly. I was at my cousin's wedding. I was a bridesmaid and I didn't know most of the people. Later, at the reception, I felt a little left out, a little envious."

"So you sneaked a glass—" he guessed.

"I sneaked two. Really put me out of it, too. I more or less embarrassed everyone. My dad had to take me home and put me to bed." She flushed, remembering.

Jack looked intrigued and understanding, too. "Was he mad at you?" he asked gently.

Lynn shook her head no, her expression sobering. "No. My mom had just died the year before. He knew I'd been having a tough time. He just told me not to try to grow up so fast and that was the end of it."

"Your dad's a wise man." Jack worked his fingers between hers, so their hands were intimately entwined.

"What about you? When, where and with whom did you have your first glass of champagne?"

Jack grinned and imparted with boyish glee, "It was New Year's Eve, my senior year in high school. My parents let me have a glass to bring in the New Year. They were having a big party. I was acting as bartender. At first, it was a real honor. I felt like quite a hotshot mixing up all those exotic drinks. Later, I began to miss my friends, wonder what I was missing by being there, working for my folks—although in their defense, it was a voluntary decision on my part. Anyway, my dad read my mood, suggested the champagne. He knew how much I wanted to be grown up and that night for the first time I felt it. Not so much because of the alcohol but because I'd been treated with dignity and respect. Know what I mean?''

"Yeah. It's a weird feeling, isn't it, when your parents treat you as an equal?''

Jack nodded, finishing his glass. "Growing up is scary.''

They looked at one another. "Do you feel grown up?'' she asked softly.

"Sometimes yes, sometimes no.''

"Same here.'' She paused. "Do you see a lot of young adults in your line of work? College students like Jessica?''

"They make up about thirty percent of my patients.''

"Is it harder to help them than older people?''

He nodded. "Generally, yes. They need so much understanding because they're at such a vulnerable age. But it's gratifying watching them grow up, begin to take responsibility for their actions, to think before they act.''

She loved his gentleness, his ability to find something to appreciate in almost everything. "You'd make a good father,'' she said softly.

His eyes held hers. "I'd like to be one someday."
His tone lowered another mesmerizing notch. "What about you?"

"I'd like to have children, too."

Jack grinned, suddenly cheered. "Sometimes it seems we have everything in common."

She batted her eyes flirtatiously. "And other times, nothing at all." Still teasing him, she got up to rummage through the picnic basket. She felt a mild buzzing in her head. The cabin was still cool, but she was definitely warm. Very warm. "I know I had a thermos of coffee packed in here somewhere."

Without warning, he was behind her, his hands on her waist. He was turning her toward him, backing her up against the counter. "Forget the coffee," he urged gently.

His arms came around her and his lips met hers in a long, soul-shattering kiss. She shuddered under the impact of it and felt spreading heat coursing through her veins. He was like a fire burning out of control, melting every shred of her resistance, each lingering doubt. Her hand moved down his back and sides, stroking, learning anew the shape of him, loving what she found.

Jack groaned as her hand passed over his groin. Her lips were parted and her breasts rose and fell with each quickened breath. Suddenly, they couldn't move fast enough, couldn't quell their impatience and the blinding need to be together now.

Jack turned, guiding them back toward the bunks. They kissed the entire way, neither of them watching where they were going, only lost in the sensual splendor of taste and touch. He bumped his shoulder against the frame, then caught the back of his knee on the bunk. ''Damn boat,'' Jack muttered, bending to turn back the sheets.

She helped him struggle out of his clothes, and she out of hers. And then they were down, twisting and turning in the cold, fresh-smelling sheets. There was none of the dreamy languor they'd experienced the first time they'd made love. Their union was all fire and urgent longing. Lynn knew her heart had never beaten so fast, her body never felt so hot and full of yearning. She knew then that he could have asked anything of her and she would have given it. But he didn't ask. Instead he gave, trapping her helplessly with intense longing until she felt completely vulnerable to someone for the first time in her life. Until she felt completely safe, free to discover and explore.

Her hands and lips became more demanding, and Jack savored her newfound boldness. Lynn was wild in ways he had never imagined—abandoned, imaginative. Every measure of passion he gave she returned, touching as he touched, kissing as he kissed.

With the rain falling softly overhead, their breath vapory in the chill of the small cabin, they crested wave after wave, taking one another to a crescendo of feeling neither dreamed existed. They were close, they were one, a bonding of heart and soul unlike anything that they had ever experienced. And Lynn knew that no matter what happened next, she would never be the same.

Chapter Thirteen

"I have some good news. I think I've found Jessica," Lynn began. It was the middle of a workday, and she'd rushed over to his office to tell him the news in person. Although he'd asked not to be involved in the tracing of his ex-patient, she knew he would want to know when she had been found.

"Where? When?" Jack looked happy but cautious.

"In New York. You know those ads we've been running in all the papers of the major cities? Well, I finally got a tip from a source I can trust." It was the man who employed Jessica in New York. Because she was working under her real name and using her own Social Security number, there was no doubt it was she.

"Have you talked to her yet?"

"No, I think that's something I'd better do in person."

"What about her parents?"

"They're going to let me handle it first. Then, if all goes well, they'll fly up to see her, too. I really think that way is best. We don't want to panic her. And since it's the Montgomerys she was running from in the first place, well, they understand the need not to push her too much too soon. At least not until we get a handle on the situation." Although Lynn's gut feeling was that everything would get resolved very soon.

"Is she all right?" Jack asked, concerned as always for his ex-patient's welfare.

Lynn nodded. "According to my source, she's very stable and is working as a waitress by day and taking acting classes at night."

Jack did a double take. "Jessica?"

"I know, it's a surprise, isn't it, considering at one time she was terrified to even get up in front of a group of people, but maybe that drama class she took turned her on to it. At any rate, I'm going to New York to talk to her this afternoon. I thought I'd let you know." Finished, she turned toward the door.

Jack caught her arm before she could leave. With courage, she met his eyes. "Are you asking me to go with you?" he asked softly.

She wanted to, but she knew it would be wrong of her to push him. "I don't want to put you on the spot."

"I know that, but I'm interested in your gut reaction here."

Lynn paused, studying his unsmiling face a moment before admitting with equal candor, in a slightly strained voice, "I don't know what I'm going to find there. I don't know what Jessica's reaction to being found will be." Lynn frowned. "I don't want to upset her, to have her run again." Maybe her instincts would serve her well in this instance and she'd do and say everything exactly right, and then maybe she wouldn't. It was a drawback, not knowing the young woman personally, as Jack did.

The silence stretched taut between them. "I can't go as a doctor, but maybe this once as a friend," Jack said finally, his expression kind. Lynn knew his main priority was to see that Jessica was all right. But he was also doing this for her. "Can you get me on your flight?" he asked softly.

A thrill of satisfaction went through her, that they'd reached a new understanding and cooperation in this. Lynn smiled. "Consider it done."

While Jack's secretary cancelled his appointments, they both went home to pack. Lynn was almost finished when the phone rang.

"I caught you at a bad time, didn't I?" Theresa guessed at the harried sound of Lynn's voice.

Lynn was rushed, but she had a few minutes to talk. "I'm getting ready to go out of town," Lynn said, snapping her suitcase shut with one hand. "One of my cases just broke."

"Where are you headed?"

Lynn picked up the telephone and carried it over to her vanity where she busied herself packing up her makeup and toiletries. "New York City."

"Good luck. Have fun and be careful."

Lynn smiled at the sober but cheerful advice. "I will," she said. "Was there any particular reason you called?" She hadn't heard from Theresa for several weeks, which was unusual, but perhaps Theresa had been as busy as she.

"Yes." Happiness bubbled up in her voice and then the words just came spilling out. "I do have some news. Remember that guy I told you about? We're getting married!"

"Oh, Theresa, I'm happy for you." She deserved a good man, and from all Theresa had told her earlier about Roy Johnson, Lynn knew he was just that.

"Thanks. You'll come to the wedding, of course." It wasn't a question but a statement.

Abruptly, Lynn had an uneasy moment, but she shook it off. There was no reason for her to feel funny around Theresa because of what she knew, any more than there would be if Theresa were a patient, and Lynn her doctor. A doctor harbored confidential information also, and put it aside. "Sure," she said finally, managing an enthusiastic tone.

"Great. It'll be two weeks from today." Theresa went on to name the time and place.

Lynn agreed to be there, then paused. "You're sure you're not moving too fast?" Theresa had decided on the artificial insemination procedure this quickly, too.

There was silence on the other end of the line, and then she heard Theresa's voice, serene and composed and very, very certain. "I love him, Lynn. More than I thought it was possible to love anyone. And he and Carter get along really well. My family likes him." She took a deep breath, as if unable to put all her thoughts into words.

Lynn's fears were vanquished. "It sounds like everything is perfect." Like Theresa had never been happier.

"It is. Well, listen, I've kept you long enough. I'll talk to you when you get back. Have fun in New York."

"I will."

Fortunately for Lynn and Jack, their flight to New York was as trouble-free as Theresa wished. They took a taxi into the city, and because it was already eight-thirty, went directly to the Actor's Workshop where Lynn had been told Jessica took classes two nights a week.

They sat in a coffee shop across from the studio. At ten o'clock, the students began filtering out of the building, and they spotted Jessica. "Let's go." Jack hurriedly paid the bill.

Together, they crossed the street and met up with Jessica at the corner. She did a double take when she saw Jack.

"Dr. Taggart," she said slowly, looking taken aback.

"Hi, Jessica. Got a minute to talk to me? Friend to friend?"

"Sure," Jessica said slowly. She looked at Lynn questioningly, then back at Jack.

"I have someone I want you to meet," Jack continued. "Jessica, Lynn O'Brien. Lynn, Jessica."

The two women shook hands. Jessica studied Lynn openly. "Are you another doctor?" In other words, what was she doing here? What were they both doing here?

"No, I'm a private investigator." Lynn reached into her pocket and withdrew a business card.

"I see." Jessica studied the card, and then looked up at Lynn. With a restless movement of her hand, she pushed back a thatch of strawberry-blond hair.

"I've been running an ad in the papers—"

"I know. Someone showed it to me a few days ago. They were amazed at the resemblance of the girl in the photo to me."

"Even when you knew I was looking for you, you didn't run again?"

For a moment, Jessica looked pained, but when she spoke her voice was serene, with an undertone of youthful resilience and defiance. "I'm through running. I'm through living in motels, being afraid someone would find me."

"I'm glad," Jack said, looking down at her. Not as a friend now, but as a former therapist.

Meeting his eyes, Jessica managed a weak smile. Lynn could see the young woman knew what a victory she'd won for herself. "Besides," Jessica continued tiredly, "I knew it would come to this eventually."

People passed them on the sidewalk. They moved back until they were standing closer to the building and out of the path of pedestrians. Jessica turned back to Lynn. "My parents hired you, didn't they?" Once again, her green eyes were alert, wary.

"Yes, they hired me."

"And Dr. Taggart? What's your part in all this?"

"Jack came because I asked him to, because I knew you trusted him," Lynn explained. "And because I didn't want to frighten you."

"My parents know I was seeing you then?" Jessica asked unhappily. Apparently that was something she would have preferred to keep quiet.

"Your sorority house forwarded a bill from my office to your parents' house," he said. "You needn't worry, your privacy has been protected. I came with Lynn today because she asked me to and because I was concerned, not so much as your doctor but as a friend. Those phone calls had me a little worried, I wasn't sure what to think."

"I'm doing fine, Doc," Jessica assured, and Lynn could see it was true. "But about my parents, are they here, too?"

"No, they're still in Indianapolis, although they'd like to see you. They're very worried."

Jessica fell silent. Lynn could see her withdrawing into herself.

"Look, why don't we take this discussion into the coffee shop across the street," Jack said. The sidewalk was too awkward a place to have that conversation.

For a moment Jessica looked as if she might resist. Jack talked to her softly, persuading. Eventually the young woman realized there could be no harm in it.

Moments later, they were all seated at a table. "I'm not surprised they tried to find me," Jessica said, putting her chin on her hand. Although initially perturbed and wary of the intrusion, because of Jack's calming presence, his assurance and protectiveness, she now seemed more relieved than anything else.

Lynn wasn't surprised. No one liked to be on the lam—for any reason or any length of time. It was too hard, keeping up the pretenses, not looking back.

"Why did you run away without telling anyone where you'd gone?" Lynn asked, noting without jealousy what a stunning beauty Jessica was in person. Her pictures didn't begin to do her justice.

"Because if my parents had known what I wanted to do with my life, they would have tried to stop me." Jessica pushed her chair away from the table. She sighed and looked at Jack tiredly, as if this were old news, before turning back to Lynn. "They wanted me to get into the family business. I want to become an actor. There's no way on this earth they would ever approve."

Lynn knew that was true where Mr. Montgomery was concerned. "I think your mother might understand," she said softly.

Jessica's lower lip jutted out petulantly. She traced the rim of her coffee cup with her thumb. "Maybe. Maybe not. She usually does what my dad tells her to do, and thinks what my father tells her to think." The last was uttered with traces of rebelliousness.

Lynn understood Jessica's frustration. She also felt Jessica was wrong. Over the past few weeks Lynn had seen Mary never being anything but determined and resilient. "Your leaving has made her stronger and she wants you back." Lynn continued to push, knowing

Jessica wasn't going to go back strictly on her own, not yet anyway.

Jessica looked up, resignation dulling her eyes. "I wish it were that easy. But it's not."

"Why did you go back to Indianapolis and then leave again?"

"You knew about that?"

"I was able to trace you, yes."

"I'd figured out what I wanted to do with my life, which was become an actress, but I was tired of running and was almost out of money." She looked at Jack and smiled. "I called you from the Atlanta airport, you know. I guess I wanted some advice."

"But you didn't ask me."

She grinned. "Maybe because I knew what you'd say. To stop running, start making my own decisions, stand by them." She grinned with youthful delight at getting the chance to repeat his words. "Anyway, I just chickened out because as broke as I was at that point, I was very tempted to go crawling back on my hands and knees."

"But you didn't," Lynn said.

"No. I almost did, though. Even went to some cheap hotel so no one would be able to find me and then went to some of my old haunts like Daisy Mae's. You know what I found out?" She looked at Jack. "That it's true what they say, you really can't go home again. I didn't fit in there anymore. I didn't want to fit in."

"So you left again."

"Yes, and came to New York. I'm not going to pretend it's been easy for me here. In fact, it's been extremely scary." She glanced at Jack. "That's why I called you again, at the office."

"Why not let your parents help you achieve your dream? Just the same way they would have helped you go through college?" Lynn asked.

Jessica's mouth took on a stubborn line. "Because I need to do this myself." She took a sip of her coffee, and then set the cup down with a thud. "By myself, for myself. I don't want anyone saying I tried to buy my way in or that only my father's connections and money enabled me to get a start. Here in New York, I'm just me. My friends are my friends, not because of what my father owns or what I'm eventually going to inherit, but because they like me just the way I am. With never any money to my name." Jessica laughed self-effacingly. "That doesn't mean I don't get discouraged at times, I do. But I'm all right."

Jessica looked at Jack, her admiration and gratitude evident. "Those sessions with you helped me to feel good about myself, to find the courage to do what I wanted to do, you know." She glanced at Lynn. "I was at a real crisis point last winter, and he helped me get through it."

Lynn was relieved to realize Jessica was indeed okay, very much in command of herself and her situation. But she also knew Jessica needed to touch base with her family, even if she didn't realize how much. And Lynn's job wouldn't be over until she had impressed that upon the young woman. "Jessica, please, call your folks. Let them know you're okay."

Jessica was silent. "They're really that worried?"

"Yes. They love you. If you need to be on your own, tell them. But at least let them know how they can reach you. Give them the chance to understand, or at least try."

The talk went on for several more minutes. Finally, Jessica saw it Lynn's way. "I guess you're right. I have been lonely without them."

Lynn smiled, glad everything was working out all right. "I know they've missed you, too."

JACK AND LYNN RETURNED to Indianapolis on the first flight out the next morning. Jessica had talked to her parents the night before on the telephone, and Lynn and Jack were encouraged. They both felt that given time, the Montgomerys would work everything out. In the meantime, the Montgomerys had promised to keep their opinions to themselves provided Jessica stay in touch. The case was over.

"Busy day for you?" Lynn said as Jack pulled his car into her driveway.

He nodded. "But I'm free for dinner. How about you? My house at eight o'clock?"

"I'll be there," Lynn promised.

She was looking forward to reveling in the conclusion of the Montgomery case, and to being together without anything hanging over them or working to push them apart. So apparently was Jack. But she didn't discover until she got to his house that evening what a wonderful, romantic evening he had planned for her. The first surprise was the roses. They were everywhere and in every color, from white to pastel pink, fragile yellow and deep red.

"Like it?" He laced an arm affectionately around her waist.

"I love it." She viewed the fragrant blossoms with a mixture of wonder and pleasure.

"Wait. There's more." He took her hand and led her into the family room. A small table and two chairs had been set up before the fireplace. It was set with his best linen and china. The crystal and silver sparkled.

Wonderful aromas wafted in from the kitchen.

"Wait," he said, before she could thank him. He clasped her hand and guided her toward the stairs. "There's more."

He led her upstairs toward the guest room. Formerly decorated with a masculine dark blue and white color scheme, the room had been transformed to a pink and white haven. Everything, from the drapes and bedspread, to the towels in the bath, had been chosen for both femininity and beauty. The closet, which had been stuffed with odds and ends before, was now bare except for a few well-chosen silk items. The bathroom was outfitted with bubble bath and soap in her favorite scent. A few silk stockings were hung over the towel rack, as well as a white silk teddy much like the one her brother Noland had destroyed and later replaced.

"You said you wanted someday to live in a totally feminine environment," he said gently. "I don't know if I could give you that, even if I tried my hardest. Pink just isn't my favorite color." She laughed at his teasing tone, and he continued seriously, "But I figured one room where you could get away even every once in a while might do a lot for your morale."

Lynn was too overcome to speak. No one had ever gone to this much trouble just to please her. Jack really did understand her, heart and soul. More importantly, he liked what he'd discovered. "All this for me?" she whispered thickly.

"I want you to be happy. As happy as you've made me," he said gently, enfolding her in his arms. He turned her to face him and gave her a long lingering kiss, letting her know how much he cared about her. She melted into him, never loving him more than at that moment. Jack was a very tender perceptive man indeed. She didn't know what she'd have done without him.

"You look happy," he murmured as they started down the stairs hand in hand.

"I am." In the family room, the fire glowed and soft romantic music played in the background. He poured them both some champagne—pink—and then brought in the meal: chicken à l'orange with fluffy white rice and delicate vegetables, followed by a dainty fruit salad. "Did you cook all this yourself?" Lynn asked after the meal was over. Her face was lit with the glow of satisfaction.

"You bet." His eyes remained unerringly on hers. The fire cast a burnished look to his dark hair, a bronze hue to his skin. "I've been planning this for days."

She couldn't resist teasing him a little. "What if I hadn't decided to come tonight?"

"Oh, I think I could have convinced you."

She was sure he could have. She knew she didn't need much persuading to agree to being with him.

He got up and walked over to her. Taking her by the hand, he led her away from the table. "I'm glad you came over tonight," he murmured as he settled next to her on the sofa. "I needed to see you, to be with you." He gently took her chin in his hand and turned her face up to his. "I love you, Lynn," he whispered, touching his lips to hers. "And I'm beginning to find out I can't live without you." He kissed her again, and then his lips blazed a fiery trail down her neck. "At least not happily anyway," he murmured, breathing in her scent.

"Oh, Jack," she whispered. "I need you, too. And I want you," her hands moved restlessly over his chest, his shoulders, to the belt at his waist. "So much . . ."

They went into her hideaway bedroom, and frantic and frenzied, then passionately deliberate and incredibly slow, they made love once and then again. It was as if they couldn't get enough of each other, as if they couldn't hold on tightly enough. And then they slept, locked in each other arms.

Hours later, Lynn woke. A glance at the clock confirmed it was after midnight—time to go home. She slipped out of bed, and Jack woke.

"Going home?" The words were spoken without inflection, yet she knew without looking at him how disappointed he was.

"My dad will worry about me if he wakes up and I'm not home."

"It's still awkward for you, isn't it, living at home?" he asked softly.

Lynn nodded slowly and sat down on the bed beside him, taking his hand in hers. "It's not just my feelings that are involved anymore. I have to think of my family. Does that sound stupid or hopelessly out-of-date?" She turned to face him worriedly.

"No. I don't like having to sneak around, either." He leaned over to kiss her reassuringly on the lips.

Lynn sighed her pleasure as the lazy kiss drew to a halt. She stood and slipped on her skirt. "As soon as I can manage it financially, I'm going to get a place of my own again." She zipped up her skirt and pulled her sweater over her head. "I love my family, but I'd like to be able to come and go as I please without having to worry about how they'll react."

"Your father would disapprove if he knew about us?" Jack asked carefully.

"He'd probably pretend not to notice, but yes, I'm sure he'd disapprove. What about yours?"

"Oh, I'm sure they'd both disapprove." Their eyes met in the soft light of his bedroom. "And they'd probably put all the blame on me."

"The old double standard," Lynn said, aware suddenly of how comfortable she felt in his home, as if she belonged there, by his side. She knew it would be all too easy to stay with him that night; she would need no encouragement at all.

Jack shrugged, still looking deep in thought. "More or less."

She emitted a lengthy sigh and then, struck by the humor of the situation, said, "Oh well." She went into his arms for a quick hug and buried her face in his chest. "Like it or not, Jack, it seems we have that in common."

"Straight-arrow parents." Jack said, lightly stroking her hair. She made a muffled sound of agreement and cuddled closer. "I guess it could be worse."

"How's that?"

"I might not have seen you tonight at all." He bent to give her another breath-stealing kiss.

"Mmm," she murmured as they drew apart. "That would have been bad."

He grinned back. "Devastating."

Jack drove her home and walked her to her door. The house was totally silent. Jack gathered her in his arms and gave her a very quiet but very sensual kiss. "See you tomorrow?" he whispered, when the languorous kiss had finally ended.

Lynn knew she was the luckiest woman on earth to have found a man like him. Destiny had thrown them together, and destiny would keep them together; she knew it in her heart. Breathlessly Lynn said, "Just try to keep me away."

Chapter Fourteen

"Lynn, did you see my new daddy? Isn't he neat?" Carter asked.

Lynn smiled down at him. He had made the perfect ring bearer for Theresa and Roy's wedding. It was also clear, by the devoted way he was clinging to his new father's hand, that he had found the male role model he needed so badly. The trio seemed perfect for each other, and having met Roy, a gentle, perceptive man in his mid-thirties, Lynn had every reason to believe that they would live happily ever after.

"Hey, why so introspective?" Jack came up to whisper in Lynn's ear.

Lynn felt herself stiffen slightly. She felt a pinprick of guilt at being caught thinking about a case that had long been closed. "I don't know. I guess I'm just a little absentminded today," she said vaguely, looking at the stacks of wedding gifts on the tables.

"Come on. I know it's more than that. You've been exceptionally quiet all day. What are you thinking about?" Jack asked.

Lynn turned toward him. She knew Jack cared about her and that made her feel cherished. "I've been thinking about you and us and just everything," Lynn answered. Truth be told, she hadn't wanted to take Jack to Theresa's wedding, but he was there when she received the invitation and Theresa specifically told her to bring a date. There was no graceful way to get out of taking Jack with her without raising his curiosity. Beyond which, she knew if she continued to see Jack, it was inevitable he and Theresa would meet someday. So, swallowing her uneasiness at having the two of them together, considering the information Lynn alone knew about Carter's paternity, she put the past aside, invited Jack, and he'd accepted.

Everything went as smoothly as Lynn had hoped. There was only one sticky moment—when she introduced Jack to Theresa and Carter. During that exchange Lynn held her breath, wondering if anyone would see the resemblance between Carter and his biological father. But to her relief no one picked up on it at all.

Jack got along well with Carter, but no better than he got along with the other children at the gathering. The simple truth of the matter was Jack liked kids, and they liked him.

"Come on, let's dance," Jack said, teasing her out of her introspective mood. "You can daydream while I hold you in my arms."

Lynn blushed. She knew she hadn't been much fun. That he was puzzled but understanding only made her feel worse, like a two-timing heel. She regretted more than ever her handling that investigation for Theresa. "I'm sorry. I just . . . I'm just a little spacey today, that's all."

"You're sure there's nothing wrong?" Jack stared down at her, his gaze affectionate.

"No, nothing." Lynn smiled determinedly and looked past his shoulder at the three-tiered cake. She wouldn't let there be.

Jack led her around the dance floor. Before she could guess what he was about, he had danced her over to a deserted corner of the reception hall. "Humor me?" he asked softly, still guiding her round and round to the beat of a soft romantic tune.

"Sure."

"Let's play a little word-association game."

Now *this* was the reason she hadn't wanted to date a psychiatrist. "Jack, no—"

"It won't be anything upsetting, I promise. Surely you're not afraid to do this?"

Yes, she was, and for a very good reason. Knowing the only way to end it was to brazen it out, she sighed resignedly and said, "Go ahead."

"Black."

Lynn took several dance steps, very aware of his arms around her. She shrugged. "I don't know. White." This was stupid.

"Weddings?"

"Happiness." Maybe if she just did it faster, he'd tire of the game sooner. Though heaven knew what he was trying to get at. . . .

"Theresa."

"That's easy. Friend."

"Carter?"

Lynn swore silently. She'd always know Jack was too perceptive for his own good. "Little boy." With effort she kept her voice even.

"Child?"

I want one of my own, was her thought. "Baby."

"Love." This came quicker.

"Need," Lynn said automatically.

"Jack Taggart."

Now that he'd mentioned his own name, she had an idea what he was fishing for—validation of her love for him. "Beau."

"Warm."

"Cozy." Like his house.

"Marriage."

"Tru—" She caught herself just in time, swallowing the last few letters of the word truth. Now she understood why psychiatrists played those games. First they bored you, then once you were relaxed they tricked you into speaking before you could think. He'd done his job well.

"Come on. Marriage," he said impatiently, wanting her to finish what she'd started.

But that she had no intention of doing. "Divorce," she amended rapidly, extricating herself from his arms.

The song hadn't ended, but he made no move to take her back into his arms. "Are you afraid of getting married again?" he asked softly, his eyes searching hers for the clue that would explain her moodiness. "Is that it?"

What could Lynn say? That she was upset because she'd had to lie to him and would have to lie to him for the rest of her life? But the past was over and done with, and the files on Theresa's case had been destroyed. She would forget she'd ever taken that case. She took a deep breath, stepping uninvited into his arms for the next dance. Jack's arms moved around her automatically, but he was still studying her intensely. "Talk to me," he murmured persuasively.

And suddenly she found there was more on her mind than she had wanted to admit. "The truth is weddings always make me feel a little melancholy."

His look gentled. "Since your divorce, you mean?"

"Always, even before I married." She shrugged. "Maybe I read too many fairy tales when I was a kid." She still wanted Prince Charming to come and sweep her away. She thought she had found him in Jack. Only now her life was too complicated for her to believe they could live in innocent love happily ever after.

He held her closer. "I know what you mean. And I understand. Weddings always put me in a strange mood, too. I'm always happy for the couple and at the same time, envious and a little sad. Wistful."

"Exactly."

He grinned, adding to the list. "Something else we have in common." He looked over at Theresa, Roy and Carter, who were preparing to cut the cake. "They do make a happy family, don't they?" he said.

Lynn nodded, relieved at the happiness she saw on their faces. "Yes, they do. They make a very happy family." And she wasn't going to do anything to spoil it. The case was closed and it would stay closed.

"WHAT DO YOU THINK? Enough potatoes? Or should I peel a few more?" Jack asked, early Thanksgiving Day.

The delicious smell of roasting turkey filled the kitchen.

"Better peel two or three more," Noland cut in, looking over Jack's shoulder. "Family rule on holidays here is to eat until you can't move."

"And suffer, working it off the rest of the year," said Sid, from his place at the kitchen sink. Since early morning, all had been actively involved in the preparation of Thanksgiving dinner.

"What do you think, fellas?" Lynn asked. "Should we have cranberry sauce and fruit salad? Or just cranberries?"

"Both," Sid said. "The guys Noland invited all eat like horses. We'll be lucky if we have anything left."

Noland shrugged. "I always hate leftovers anyway."

"Hey, that turkey casserole I make is good," Lynn countered.

Sid grinned and patted his middle. "You don't have to tell me. My mouth is watering already just thinking about it."

Noland shook his head in disgust—he hated casseroles of any kind, always had. "You two deserve each other."

Jack put the potatoes on the stove and turned the burner on low. "What's left to do? Want me to set the table?"

"Sure," Lynn said, going to the refrigerator for more fruit.

"The tablecloth's in the linen closet down the hall," Noland said. "No, not there. That's the sewing room."

"Jack!" Lynn shouted, racing down the hall after him. "Don't go in there" her voice trailed off weakly when she saw it was too late. He was already in there and she knew what he'd find.

He came out, holding up a dark blue sweater just his size. "I didn't know you knew how to knit." It was all finished except for the trim at the bottom.

"Uh, she didn't. Gail taught her," Noland said casually. Then taking a second look at the sweater Jack was holding, he swore.

"What?" Jack said.

"That's your Christmas present you're holding up. Lynn's been working on it for weeks."

"Noland!" Lynn cried, exasperated beyond belief.

"Hey, he's no dummy, he would've figured it out," Noland said. Then reading the look on his sister's face, he quietly excused himself and left the room.

Jack came toward her. "This is for me?" he asked in an emotional whisper.

The heat of embarrassment flooded her face; Lynn knew her cheeks must be scarlet. "Well, yes. I—I hadn't made up my mind to give it to you definitely yet. I wanted to make sure it turned out all right. But it did so I guess, yes, it'll be yours when I finish. Which should be in just a few weeks."

"When did you make up your mind to do this?"

"It was after we saw those hand-knit sweaters at the festival, when you told me how much those sweaters used to mean to you."

"Do you know that's the sweetest thing anyone has ever done for me, ever?" Jack whispered, incredibly touched.

Lynn blushed again and felt an incredible warmth wrapping around her heart. "I could only hope so," she whispered back, tilting her face up to his.

Jack's lips touched hers, in a kiss that was both binding and tender. *This,* she thought, *this is forever. It's how true love feels.*

Only the sound of a throat clearing from the doorway stopped them. "Hey, come on, you two, break it up," Noland grinned good-naturedly. "You can neck later. Right now, we've got a table to set."

Lynn smiled. This was going to be the best holiday season yet.

The day passed swiftly, hurried on by the rowdy guests—all men since her brother and father hadn't thought to invite a single female. Jack fit right in and enjoyed the bustling good cheer every bit as much as everyone. Nonetheless, there were several times Lynn saw her brother drift off into thought. Later that evening, when they were alone in the kitchen, she asked him about it. "How are you doing?"

"What do you mean, how am I doing?" Noland asked as he refilled the ice trays one by one. "I'm great."

"Really, Noland. The truth."

He stopped what he was doing and turned to face her, a grim look on his face. "You mean do I miss Gail? Sure I miss her."

Lynn let out a slow breath, relaxing at the calm acceptance she saw on his face. "It really is over, isn't it?" she said. Even though the divorce had been finalized legally, she hadn't accepted it until that moment when she saw that Noland had.

"Yeah, Lynn, it's over. You know what Dad used to say when we were growing up, that there's no education like adversity. Well, I think he's right. Gail and I were never meant to be together. I shouldn't have married her. I know now that if I ever get married again, and I imagine one of these days I will, that whoever I marry is going to have to understand and accept from the very beginning how much I love my work. I know there's danger, but look at me, I got shot just going to the store for a carton of milk."

"I know. You're better off knowing how to protect yourself. And we're all better off because you're there."

"So you're giving up the matchmaking business forever?" he asked hopefully.

Lynn nodded, feeling a few tears gather in her eyes. She was sad for Noland, for what he'd lost. Because he hurt, she hurt, too. But she knew he was already starting to make plans for the future. As soon as his house sold, he and Gail were going to split the equity, and he was going to buy a townhouse and be out on his own again. "I never meant to be a pain in the ass. I just wanted to make it better for you." She wanted him to have someone special in his life.

He held out his arms to her, and she went to him. "Lynn, you've got to stop trying to protect me. I'm the big brother, I should be trying to protect you."

She sniffed and pulled away from him, blinking back her tears. It was the holiday season getting to her, that was all. "I can take care of myself."

"Yeah, well I can take care of myself, too. So can Dad. So, we're all set." He paused. "Seriously, Lynn, you've got to stop feeling so responsible for other people. If someone makes a mistake, it's theirs to live with, not yours. Not even if you know about it beforehand. You're responsible for you, that's it. That's all."

"I wish it were that easy," she confessed, "but when I see someone in trouble—"

Noland grinned and finished for her, "You just want to help."

"Right."

"Well, I guess you're in the right profession, hmm? I don't know of anything else than P.I. work where nosiness comes in so handy."

She thumped him playfully on the chest. "You really are a rat."

"Yeah." He grinned back, not the least bit offended. "I know."

"Everything okay in here?" Jack asked, coming into the kitchen. Noland excused himself and went out.

"Everything's great," Lynn said, feeling markedly cheered. "Noland and I were just working out a few kinks in our relationship."

"Good." His eyes darkened visibly. "Want to go for a drive?"

"Where?"

"I don't know." He shrugged. "Somewhere dark and quiet—"

That sounded like heaven, Lynn thought. "No brothers?"

"No football. No wall-to-wall people."

"Sounds good to me." She smiled and kissed him quickly. "Just let me get my coat."

"I ENJOYED BEING at your house for Thanksgiving," Jack said as they strolled hand in hand inside the covered bridge. Moonlight filtered down through the trees. The air was crisp and cold, which was very welcome after a day spent indoors.

"It was fun having you there."

He gave her a crooked smile and stopped walking, pivoting to face her. "You mean I'm growing on you?"

She gripped his hand tighter. "More than that, silly." She didn't think there were words to explain the depth of her feelings for him. "You constantly surprise me," she said softly. "For instance, I never would have guessed when I first met you how romantic you are."

"Because I insisted on coming back to the covered bridge where we had our first formal date?"

"I wouldn't have expected it, tonight of all nights." When they'd started driving, he refused to tell her where they were going. But as they neared Parke County, she figured it out. And he was right, it was a great place to go—to walk and think and remember. She fell in love with him here. She sensed he felt the same—that everything that had developed in the past few months had really started here on the day they first glimpsed the real people beneath the surface affability.

"You looked like you'd had quite enough football and turkey for one day," he said.

"True," Lynn answered, sighing. Noland and his friends were great, but too much of them at any one time got on her nerves. Jack had sensed that and moved to free them both. How was it possible he could see so easily into her? she wondered. How had she ever managed to live her life without him?

He kissed her tenderly and then held her close. "I was going to save this for Christmas. I had it all planned out. How I would prepare you for some great big present and then show up with this little tiny box, small enough to fit in my pocket."

Lynn's heart raced, as she anticipated what he was going to say.

"I can't live without you. Well, I can," he amended dryly with a boyish grin, before his eyes turned serious again, "but I don't want to." His voice deepened with the force of the emotion he was feeling, "Marry me, Lynn. I promise you I'll do everything in my power to make you happy."

"You've already made me happy," she sighed, feeling the last of the shadows around her heart disappear. Finally, she had a future again; *they* had a future.

"I do love you," he said softly, moving his mouth over hers, devouring its softness.

Standing on tiptoe, she returned his slow, mesmerizing kiss. As he roused her passion, his own grew stronger.

"And I love you." She was blissfully happy, fully alive.

He grinned, an expression of deep contentment in his eyes. His hands moved beneath her coat, to skim her waist and hips, and pull her more fully against him. "Is that a yes?" he asked in a low, mellow tone.

Lynn knew she'd never wanted anything or anyone more. Their union had a feeling of rightness about it. "Yes," she whispered. "Yes, I'll marry you."

He held her to him and a delicious shudder coursed through her body. "You've just made me the happiest man on earth," he whispered in her ear.

That went for both of them, Lynn thought.

Chapter Fifteen

"Hey, thanks for letting me use your computer," Jack said several days later.

Lynn glanced admiringly down at the diamond engagement ring sparkling on her left hand. Jack hadn't wasted any time presenting her with it. The moment the jewelry stores opened on Friday morning, he had her trying on rings. And not just any ring would do. They must have looked at twenty different styles before they finally decided on a simple but elegant solitaire, the gold band etched with a leaf design.

"Anytime."

"Now if I can just figure out how to use it," Jack said. He was accustomed to working on a different model.

"It's not as hard as it looks, though I'm hardly an expert," Lynn said, walking into the kitchen to pour them both a cup of coffee. She returned and stared distractedly out the window at the morning sunshine, then catching herself daydreaming, turned back to Jack. There was a strength in his face, a confident set to his shoulders—and frown lines on his forehead.

Poor guy, she thought. He looked most unhappy, faced with a strange computer.

"First you have to call up the menu," she said, joining him. She looked over his shoulder to make sure he'd typed in the right command. "Yeah. Now, type in the name of your document."

He punched in a few letters. Without warning, he began to laugh. He squinted up at her. "Is this some kind of joke?"

Lynn, who'd been looking out the window and daydreaming about their impending marriage again, turned back abruptly. "What?"

"You've already got a file on me."

Lynn paled. That was impossible! She'd already erased the files on Jack and Theresa. And she'd given him a brand new diskette to use, one straight from the package.

"You're joking, right?" She moved so she could see the screen and paled even more as she read the message next to the blinking cursor. It said a Jack Taggart file already existed.

She bit down on an oath. "This must be a mistake." She started to reach for the keyboard to delete the file, but Jack blocked her way. "Oh, no," he said, reading the menu and pushing a few buttons. "This I've got to see."

Over her protests he had called his file up onto the screen. Two clicks of the keys later and he was reading the file. It began with standard surveillance information.

Again, Lynn tried to reach forward to delete the information before he could see or discover. Catching her arms behind her, still sure it was some kind of a joke, he pulled her down on his lap and held her captive despite her furious struggles to extricate herself.

In seconds, he had read enough to realize she'd had him followed and that there was a marked resemblance to his "son," four-year-old Carter Richards. His expression shell-shocked, he released her. She got up slowly and moved away, knowing it would be pointless to try and delete the information now—he'd never let her do it. Much as she wanted to, she couldn't overpower him or undo what had just happened, what he'd seen.

The silence in the room was deafening. Jack stared at the screen, glanced at her, hurt and disbelief in his eyes, then back at the screen. Lynn was numb and shaking. *Oh, God,* she thought, *I don't believe this is happening. All my worst nightmares have come true.*

"You want to explain this?" Jack said grimly at last, pushing his chair away from the computer console and stalking toward her.

Lynn swallowed hard, nailed to the spot by his judgmental stare. It was all over between them; she saw it in his face. "I—I don't know how it happened," she stammered nervously, holding back bitter tears of mortification and distress. "I erased all that information." She searched her mind for a logical explanation. "I was just learning to use my computer when I worked on your case. I must have inadvertently entered the information on the hard disk inside the computer.''

''I don't mean that,'' Jack snapped impatiently. His face moved closer to hers, his expression stony. ''I could care less why the information just came on screen. I want to know why you were investigating me!'' His eyes narrowed to slits as he looked down at her.

Lynn took a deep breath and she explained briefly in a shaking voice. ''Don't you see?'' she finished emotionally, knowing she hadn't touched him in the slightest. ''I had to take the case!''

''Like hell you did!'' he growled.

Anger stiffened Lynn's spine. ''If I hadn't done it, someone else would've!''

''Was meeting me part of the deal?'' he asked in a voice that vibrated with rage.

''No. The case was already wrapped up by then!'' She moved away from him defensively, hugging her arms to her middle. ''It was an accident. I was passing out flyers in your building.''

Jack stared at her for a long while, weighing everything she said. ''That's why you backed away from me the first time we met, why you were so nervous, isn't it?'' he accused, his lips thinning to a hard white line. ''Why you were so reluctant to date me. Isn't it, Lynn?'' He stalked closer when she didn't answer and grabbed her wrist when she would have turned away. *''Isn't it?''*

''Yes! All right! Yes, it was!''

The hand on her wrist tightened. Betrayal was stamped on his face. "Dammit, Lynn, you and your meddling!" he said in a low voice thick with fury.

Having no defense, she stood there, crying and shaking, hurting more than she'd ever hurt in her life.

Suddenly, he whitened. "Does Theresa know about this?"

"No," Lynn said with agitation. "I was hired only to get information on the donor's health. No name was ever mentioned, nor did she want one. She only wanted reassurance that Carter had nothing to fear healthwise. When the case was closed, I destroyed everything."

His blue eyes were icy. "Not quite everything," his lips curled bitterly.

"Jack—"

"Don't." He put up a weary hand to stop her, before she could say another word. "Don't try and ask me to forgive you for this. Because I can't. And I don't think I ever will!"

Chapter Sixteen

Jack ran along the shores of the lake, mindless of the cold or the punishment he was inflicting on his body. He'd gone out there knowing he had to be alone, away from everything and everyone. He intended to take his boat out on the lake, but one look at the houseboat and he knew that, too, was ruined for him now. All he could think of was how passionately he and Lynn had made love there, and the fact it was never, ever, going to happen again.

Their relationship was over.

Not because he wanted it to be but because he had no choice but to break it off. It wasn't just the fact she'd investigated him or that she hadn't told him she'd done so. He understood and accepted professional ethics. But what she'd done for Theresa went miles beyond professional ethics. It was a complete invasion of privacy, meddling in the worst possible sense. She'd looked for the donor knowing she could be destroying lives, and yet she'd done so anyway. He couldn't forgive Lynn for that, for not knowing when and where to draw the line.

If only it didn't hurt so damn much, Jack thought, pausing to wipe the moisture from his face. Misty rain poured down from the sky. His breath puffed out in the cold winter air.

Numbness went through him, soul-deep. He felt chilled from head to toe, tense as a taut wire. Stupid as it was, part of him just didn't want to believe that she'd done it, but the evidence had been before him on that infernal computer screen. And now that he knew, there was no going back, no easy way out. They both had to live with what she'd uncovered. Damn her, he thought on a renewed burst of anger and resentment.

"WHAT'S GOING ON with you and Jack?" Sid asked his daughter gently several days later.

"Simply put," Lynn said tightly, "the wedding's off."

"You're sure?" Sid finished the dinner dishes and moved to sit beside Lynn at the kitchen table.

Lynn toyed with her coffee, knowing she wouldn't be able to drink any of it. She hadn't been able to eat or drink much since the breakup. She couldn't remember ever feeling this depressed or bereft since her mother's death; it was as if she'd lost the best part of herself.

Half of her knew it was all her fault, the other half said Jack should have at least tried to understood the impossible situation she'd been in with Theresa. Yes, she knew she had made a mistake ever agreeing to track down Carter's father. But she had, and it was over.

"Have you tried to meet with him, talk things through?"

"I suggested it several times," Lynn said sadly. "But he won't even talk to me." She was embarrassed to have her father see the unshed tears that were blurring her vision. "He has his answering machine on at home, and he has instructed his secretary not to put me through at work."

"I'm sorry."

"So am I," Lynn said morosely. More so than anyone knew.

"Maybe you'll work things out yet," Sid said hopefully.

Lynn sighed, and restless, got up to pace the kitchen. She felt like crying and it was all she could do to keep the tears at bay. She swallowed hard around the lump in her throat, not holding out much hope for a reconciliation. "I don't think that'll happen, Dad." She'd seen the look on Jack's face. As far as he was concerned the moment he had seen the information on the computer screen, it was over.

"Did you do something to make him angry?" Sid asked curiously, trying to understand.

Lynn sighed and raked her hands through her hair. "Yes. He found out, inadvertently, that I had investigated him for a client. The case is long over now."

"But he's angry because you kept this from him?" Sid asked sympathetically.

Lynn nodded.

"If you were investigating him, why did you go out with him in the beginning?"

"Because the case was closed. And he was so persistent, and then there was the business with Jessica Montgomery." They'd been thrown together at every turn. The rest had just happened, as if their romance had been destined. "Dad, I know how complex the situation is. I know I would've been better off never meeting him, but I did, and our affection for one another just kind of snowballed until neither of us could ignore it anymore." Tears blurred her eyes and she determinedly blinked them back. "I couldn't help falling in love with him." Just like she couldn't help the emptiness inside her now.

"There was no way you could've told him you'd investigated him in the past?"

Lynn shook her head, wiping the moisture from her face with the back of her hand. "How could I? If I'd done that, I would've been violating a client's right to privacy."

Sid's brows furrowed. "Has Jack done anything wrong?"

"No, of course not. It was, is, a personal matter. For a client," Lynn sniffed. Anything more she couldn't say.

"Does that mean this situation, whatever it was, is still ongoing?" her dad asked gently.

He took in her silence and said, "I guess that answers my question. Look, Jack always seemed like a reasonable fella to me, and I know how you get when you're on a case, Lynn. Sometimes you think the end justifies the means. Is this what happened in the investigation of Jack, too? Did you get carried away?"

Maybe in taking the case, she thought, because she'd known it would be troublesome from the start. "He thinks I never should have accepted the job in the first place."

"Is he right?"

"No. Yes. I don't know," Lynn said tiredly, sinking back down into her chair. She'd never felt so tired and defeated in her life. She didn't know how she was ever going to square this with her conscience. Or make it up to Jack. Because the information he had now wasn't just something that could be erased or forgotten. How well she had learned that! There was a reason for complete anonymity, and she wished in retrospect she had respected that and abided by the rules. Because if she had, Lynn thought, she wouldn't be in the mess she was now. She wouldn't have lost the love and friendship of the best man she had ever known. She knew she had only herself to blame.

"I WANT TO arrange a meeting," Jack told Lynn.

She stared at him in stupefaction. She wasn't sure what he had wanted when he'd asked her to meet him at his office late Wednesday evening. She'd half hoped he might want a reconciliation, but the look on his face crushed her hopes.

"What are you talking about?" she asked in a trembling voice.

"With Carter and Theresa."

Lynn paled to the color of parchment. Without warning, her hands began to shake. "You can't do that. You can't possibly—"

"Are you going to do it or am I?" She said nothing in response, merely stared at him mutinously. In a voice that grated on her nerves, he continued, "Of course if I do it I'll probably end up having to tell her the truth."

"You're serious about this," she whispered hoarsely.

"Carter is my son." His jaw was rigid with determination. "Now that I know that..." his voice trailed off emotionally.

Desperately, Lynn held on to the shreds of her composure and tried to reason with him, "Jack, you can't tell him you're his father. You and Theresa signed agreements that guaranteed anonymity."

"An agreement you've already broken once," Jack said stubbornly, determined to obtain his peace of mind regarding Carter's welfare.

Pausing to get a grip on the desolation she felt, she said with icy deliberateness, "I won't help." She wouldn't put herself in an untenable, unethical situation again. She had more than learned her lesson the last time!

He shrugged. "If that's your choice, then fine, I'll do it my way."

His low determined tone filled her with sudden panic. He was grimly serious. Lynn thought of Theresa's wedding, how happy she and Carter had been. Her stomach was still clenched tight.

She stared at him mutinously, realizing at last that she had no way out of the tangled web her sleuthing had created. "Some choice."

"HAVING A HOLIDAY GET-TOGETHER was a wonderful idea," Theresa said as she welcomed Lynn and Jack into her home several days later.

"I agree," Roy said. "I've been wanting to get better acquainted with Theresa's friends. Now that we're settled in, we plan to do a lot more entertaining." Both he and Theresa looked supremely happy. The house was festively adorned for the holidays. Christmas carols played softly on the stereo.

"Did you see our Christmas tree?" Carter asked Lynn. "Isn't it pretty?"

"It sure is, honey. Did you decorate it yourself?" She smiled down into his beaming face.

"Me and Mommy and Daddy decorated it together!" he reported with exuberance.

"Carter, why don't you show Jack and Lynn the decorations you made at school?" Theresa suggested as she passed around a tray of homemade canapés.

"Okay!" Carter walked over to the tree and with utmost care, removed the colorful decorations he had made. He brought them over to the sofa where Jack and Lynn sat, and promptly launched into a detailed description of how he had made the papier-mâché angel and the multicolored felt Santa Claus. Lynn was amazed at how talkative he was, how at ease. He'd always been shy around adults, but apparently Roy's presence was helping him lose his reticence.

Jack listened attentively, smiling as Carter expressed his joy over his accomplishment. "Do you like school?" he asked pleasantly. To Lynn's relief, nothing of Jack's other emotions showed. Whatever else he was feeling inside, he was keeping very well contained.

"Oh, yes." Carter nodded vigorously. "We do lots of fun things!"

"They went on a field trip to a bakery and got to see how bread was made, and they also went to the Children's Museum," Theresa added, coming back into the room with a handful of cocktail napkins and a glass of milk for her son.

"We saw dinosaurs!" Carter explained.

Roy passed out glasses of the hot wassail punch he'd made. "I'm going to chaperone on the next trip. They're going to the planetarium."

"My daddy's been teaching me all about stars!" Carter hopped off the sofa. Walking over to stand beside Roy, he laced his hand affectionately through Roy's. There was no denying the love flowing between the two, Lynn thought. Carter had welcomed Roy into his life every bit as willingly and enthusiastically as his mother.

"I've got a telescope," Roy explained to their guests.

"Let's show Jack and Lynn!" Carter cried excitedly. "Oh, Daddy, can we? Please?"

Roy looked hesitantly at the adults. "We'd be interested," Jack assured, and for the next half an hour, the four adults shared Carter's wonderment over the constellations.

Dinner went just as smoothly. By the time they got ready to leave several hours later, Lynn had no doubt in her mind that Theresa had finally found the happiness that had been denied her earlier. Roy and Carter were equally content. It wasn't so easy to figure out what Jack was thinking, though, or to guess what he would do next.

She knew he blamed her for the whole mess. And she knew he was right to do so. He'd been through purgatory because of her. Looking back, she realized now that she should have found some way to talk Theresa out of the investigation or at least found some ethical way to do it. Through the hospital where the insemination was done, perhaps. Instead, because she was so eager to prove her mettle as a private detective, and because she was looking for the quickest way to set her friend's mind at ease, she made a colossal mistake. A mistake that cost Jack and herself countless pain.

She didn't know what Jack was going to do now, or if he would ever be able to find it in his heart to forgive her. Suddenly she knew she had to try to win him back. They'd shared too much for her just to let him go. Somehow, she would talk to him and make him listen.

The moment they were out of Theresa's door and heading down the walk to his car, she turned to him and said, "I have to talk to you."

"I agree," he responded, looking at her, an unreadable expression on his face. "But not here. Someplace private," he said after a long moment. "My house?"

It was a start. Still unable to read his intentions, Lynn nodded her agreement.

It took all of her willpower to remain silent on the short ten-minute drive to his home, but somehow she managed. "About Carter," she said, her heart pounding as he unlocked his front door and ushered her inside.

"I know he's happy. I saw that tonight."

Lynn stared at him, her knees trembling badly. "Does that mean you won't claim him?" she asked cautiously, almost afraid to hope.

He took her coat from her shoulders and hung it on the rack in the hall. "Yes," he nodded solemnly, his voice low and underscored with regret. "I think I knew from the start that not claiming him would be the best, but I needed to be sure I was doing the right thing, that he is well taken care of." Jack paused and took a minute to get a handle on his emotions. He swallowed hard. "Carter is well loved—I'm not selfish enough to upset that." His eyes glistened with moisture as he looked at Lynn, everything he felt for the child on his face. "I'd be lying though if I said I didn't intend to keep tabs on him. He may not need me to be his father, but he can always use a guardian angel, someone extra looking out for him, making sure from a distance that everything's okay."

Lynn emitted a slow breath. Tears glistened in her eyes, too. She knew how hard this was for Jack, what a sacrifice he was making, and how much it was costing him. Right now he looked so vulnerable it made her heart ache. "For what it's worth," she said in a voice thick with tears, "I think you're doing the right thing."

"So do I."

They lapsed into silence rippling with unspoken emotions. Then both spoke at once.

"Lynn—"

"Before you say anything, let me talk." She held up a hand, cutting off his words. "I need to apologize, to tell you how sorry I am. You were right. What I did for Theresa went far beyond meddling, and I'll never ever do anything that foolhardy again. The stakes—people's emotions—are too high." He looked relieved and she continued in a cautioning voice, "I can't promise I won't sometimes go that extra mile, because I will. But I also know now that there are some situations I just have to leave alone, and some rules that should never be broken."

A relieved smile on his face, he took her hand in his. "I know you do what you do because you genuinely care about people and you want to help."

"You forgive me then?"

Jack nodded, his eyes never leaving hers. His hand tightened over hers. "I've been thinking a lot the past few days. I realized one of the things I always liked best about you was your devotion to your family and friends. The work you do—specializing in delicate family matters—isn't easy but it's very important." His voice roughened with emotion, he murmured urgently, "Lynn, I want us to start over again."

For a moment she was too stunned to speak. Then relief washed over her in waves. "Oh, Jack, I want that, too." She went into his arms, cherishing the warmth they shared, his strength.

He kissed her tenderly, "I love you, Lynn."

"And I love you." She hugged him back tightly. "Oh, Jack, I know we'll never agree on everything. I'm always going to be too impetuous, but I'm not going to do anything illegal or unethical in the course of an investigation ever again. I promise you that."

"I know you don't take any of this lightly, that you always do the best you can in any situation, and that the past few months have been hard on you because you do want to help so much." He knew she hadn't done anything to hurt anyone deliberately.

She leaned into him, savoring his warmth and his strength, thinking of all they'd been through. "I'm sorry I caused you so much pain."

Jack shrugged, willing to let the past be just that. A hand beneath her chin, he tilted her face up to his. Understanding and forgiveness softened the lines of his face, along with the knowledge of his own part in their break-up. "Something good comes out of everything. For the first time I understand the primal urge to nurture and protect one's young. I also know now how much I want children of my own—with you. And I know how much I miss not having you in my life." Lowering his head, he kissed her gently at first, then with building passion. "Marry me, Lynn."

She stood very still, basking in her joy. Then tears of happiness sliding down her face, she agreed. "Yes. Oh, yes, I will."

His happiness evident, he released her just long enough to retrieve the diamond ring she'd returned. With him assisting tenderly, she slid the diamond onto her finger. It felt so right. She'd been right—destiny was on their side. "You know something? I think we are a perfect match," she said softly, as his lips brushed her knuckles, and then her palm.

He took her into his arms for another lingering heartfelt kiss. "Lady," he murmured gently, "I agree."

Harlequin American Romance

COMING NEXT MONTH

#281 ONE WHIFF OF SCANDAL by Judith Arnold

For weeks Griff had been on the trail of the worst sex, money and power scandal ever to hit sleepy Rhode Island towns. Then Jill Bergland stumbled onto the story and made Griff wonder—could love survive scandal?

#282 KISSED BY AN ANGEL by Kathy Clark

Guilt had changed Kristi Harrison's life and made her seek solitude at a Florida beach house. When nightmares drove her from her bed to the quiet of the moonlit beach, she met Scott Sanders, who was driven by his own midnight demons. They each had their secret guilt—but could they find peace in each other's arms?

#283 SIDE BY SIDE by Muriel Jensen

As children, Janessa and Clay had promised to be united forever. It was a bond they vowed would never be broken. But could their childhood dreams anticipate their adult realities?

#284 LADY'S CHOICE by Linda Randall Wisdom

Whoever called it "midlife crisis" was right! At forty, Abby's life had gone haywire. Her grown children continued to give her problems, and now her best friend suddenly decided he wanted *more* than friendship. Zach's timing was perfect, for they would need their combined strength to weather the crisis to come.

Harlequin Temptation dares to be different!

Once in a while, we Temptation editors spot a romance that's truly innovative. To make sure *you* don't miss any one of these outstanding selections, we'll mark them for you.

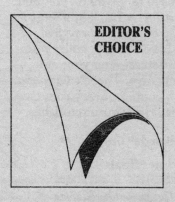

EDITOR'S CHOICE

When the ''Editors' Choice'' fold-back appears on a Temptation cover, you'll know we've found that extra-special page-turner!

THE *Temptation*

EDITORS

Have You Ever Wondered If You Could Write A Harlequin Novel?

Here's great news—Harlequin is offering a series of cassette tapes to help you do just that. Written by Harlequin editors, these tapes give practical advice on how to make your characters—and your story—come alive. There's a tape for each contemporary romance series Harlequin publishes.

Mail order only

All sales final

- -

TO: *Harlequin Reader Service*
      Audiocassette Tape Offer
      P.O. Box 1396
      Buffalo, NY   14269-1396

I enclose a check/money order payable to HARLEQUIN READER SERVICE® for $9.70 ($8.95 plus 75¢ postage and handling) for EACH tape ordered for the total sum of $_____*
Please send:

☐ Romance and Presents   ☐ Intrigue
☐ American Romance   ☐ Temptation
☐ Superromance   ☐ All five tapes ($38.80 total)

Signature_____
                                    (please print clearly)
Name:_____
Address:_____
State:_____ Zip:_____

*Iowa and New York residents add appropriate sales tax.   AUDIO-H